M000313794

Snowflake on a Spider's Web

by

Patti Laughlin Fogt

DORRANCE
PUBLISHING CO
EST. 1920
PITTSBURGH, PENNSYLVANIA 15238

The contents of this work, including, but not limited to, the accuracy of events, people, and places depicted; opinions expressed; permission to use previously published materials included; and any advice given or actions advocated are solely the responsibility of the author, who assumes all liability for said work and indemnifies the publisher against any claims stemming from publication of the work.

All Rights Reserved
Copyright © 2021 by Patti Laughlin Fogt

No part of this book may be reproduced or transmitted, downloaded, distributed, reverse engineered, or stored in or introduced into any information storage and retrieval system, in any form or by any means, including photocopying and recording, whether electronic or mechanical, now known or hereafter invented without permission in writing from the publisher.

Dorrance Publishing Co
585 Alpha Drive
Pittsburgh, PA 15238
Visit our website at *www.dorrancebookstore.com*

ISBN: 978-1-6376-4333-4
eISBN: 978-1-6376-4645-8

Table of Contents

Chapter One

Dance of the Mayflies

Popular Music from 1939:
"Somewhere Over the Rainbow" Judy Garland
"Strange Fruit" Billie Holiday
History: The Dual Alliance was an alliance between Austria-Hungary and Germany, which was created by treaty on October 7, 1879 as part of Germany's Otto von Bismarck's system of alliances to prevent war.

Eva was daydreaming again. She was finishing her chores at her grandparents' kosher butcher shop in Tokaj, Hungary.

"Eva, if you don't stop daydreaming, you'll never get to the river to paint what you're daydreaming about," Mama, her grandmother, lovingly scolded as she was leaving the butcher shop for the day. She stepped into the attached kitchen of their home. Work was done in the shop for the day except for Eva's chores.

"Yes, Mama," Eva said with a lilt in her voice because she knew Mama was right.

Eva had always been a dreamer. She had to be to survive. It had become her protection that she used since she lost her parents at two years old. Watercolor painting was the only thing she found to delve into to escape from the pain and loss. It freed her soul like nothing else could.

The scent of wild lilacs, washed by the late spring rain, drifted over the vineyards, like a silk scarf blowing unencumbered in the wind. The lightly scented breeze floated into the open windows of the butcher shop. It was drawing Eva's interests outside like the Pied Piper.

Eva hurried to finish her chores. She scrubbed diligently. Washing down the countertops with the well-worn cotton towels and chlorine, she worked hard but dreamed of distant, enchanted cities like Paris.

Cleaning and closing had become her responsibility at the end of the day. Her bib overalls were splattered by chlorine so much that it had worn the fabric thin in some areas. She did not mind. Her apron covered most of the thin areas. She was not vain. She never thought about her stunning looks. Her dreams meant more to her than her shimmering, long, black, curly hair and her ice-blue eyes. Her olive skin was just like her mother's. Her smile reminded her grandparents of her father.

Mama and Papa loved to make her smile and laugh. Her laugh was contagious. Her sense of humor was ornery and quick. They never knew what she was going to say or do to make their day a little brighter.

The shop closes at noon on Fridays to prepare for Shabbat. Mama's goulash had been simmering in a huge iron pot on the large woodstove for hours. Mama made goulash for Eva's eighteenth birthday dinner. The smell of paprika was scrumptiously in the air. Mama had made Eva's favorite dessert, Dobos cake. They would celebrate as soon as Eva returned from painting by the river.

Papa was at their barnyard. He was within earshot of both Eva and Mama, feeding the chickens, cows, and Lucy, their large, black, now-graying draft horse. Papa was closing the barn for the day.

Eva loved working with her grandparents. However, painting down by the river was her favorite escape. She had built an area with sticks, stones, mud, and branches where she could go to her secluded hideaway by the Tisza River to dream and paint uninterrupted.

"Mama… Papa… I'm done," Eva yelled to both grandparents, while taking her tattered, bloodstained apron off. Throwing it into the laundry basket, she shut the windows and shutters and ran into the kitchen to give Mama a kiss on the cheek before she left.

"Be home early, sweetheart. It is Shabbat," Mama instructed. "I've got something special for your birthday."

"Ooohhh, what is it?" Eva said as she took Mama by the hands and began to dance with her to the sound of the bubbling, steaming goulash. Its lid was popping up and down on the large pot. The hissing and crackling sound of the wood in the belly of the stove made it sort of a symphony in their cozy little kitchen.

"You'll find out when you get home," Mama laughed.

Eva twirled Mama like a ballroom dancer, letting her go gently to the far side of the kitchen. Then she went to the stove and hovered over the goulash.

"It smells great, Mama," Eva complimented as she grabbed the potholders to lift the lid.

Closing her eyes, she inhaled the delicious simmering feast. Smelling its savory flavor, it was as if it was a royal meal fit for a queen. She hurriedly took a huge wooden spoonful of the delicious, paprika-spiced goulash into her mouth without blowing on it. She was trying to not get caught cheating on dinner. She blew on it while it was in her mouth. She should have known better. It was steaming hot. She grasped her hand over her mouth so she would not spit it out, quickly tossed the spoon down, and threw the lid back on the pot. She mumbled to herself that she should not have done that. She dashed to the door to get her backpack full of homemade art supplies off its hook, threw it around her shoulders, while still trying to swallow the scorching mouthful.

"Burned your tongue, didn't you?" Mama asked with a knowing grin, snapping her on the butt with the end of the kitchen towel.

"Yes, Mama, ouch," she mumbled and smiled, trying to swallow the piping-hot mouthful. "Gotta go. Love you. Great goulash, Mama." She waved as she ran out the door. Eva was trying to hurry so she could catch a glimpse of the famous Tisza River mayflies that she had been dreaming about painting since last mayfly season.

Mama just laughed at her and shook her head as she watched Eva spring out the door like a gazelle being chased by a lion.

"Some of our customers said there was a big crowd down at the bridge waiting to see the mayflies today," Papa yelled as he patted Lucy on the neck. He called out to Eva as she ran down the old volcanic gravel path that led through the vineyards and through the meadow down to the Tisza.

"Wonderful, Papa," she yelled back, as she tugged to tighten her backpack straps that he had made for her. He and Mama had made most of her art supplies too.

Eva ran through the flower-filled meadow. Its kaleidoscope colors of wildflowers were singing a chorus of light and shadow to her artistic mind. She adored the wildflowers she passed while running on the deer path. She thought, if only she could render a painting as sweet as Monet did, she would be the happiest artist in the world. He had always been her favorite artist.

Papa listened to her voice as it faded away on the breeze. He watched her run toward her private studio on the steep bank. His heart swelled with pride at what a wonderful young lady she has turned out to be. He only wished his daughter and son-in-law could have been here to watch her grow up. Eva faded into the distance with her long black curly hair flying in the wind as she ran down the well-worn path.

Papa wondered about her future. Who would she marry? If she would marry? What would this impending war bring? He and Mama worried. They also knew she was strong and could handle anything.

Papa finished his work in the barn. He went the few meters to the house and called out, "Opal," he spoke with a little spunkiness in his voice.

"Lawrence, wipe your feet. I smell barn," warned Opal with a loving grin.

"I will take my boots off at the door as always my love," Papa answered with a bit of exhilaration in his voice. He took Mama by the waist and right hand and danced her around the kitchen in his stocking feet, as if they had just met.

Opal laughed her hearty laugh that he loved to hear, "Oh, Lawrence, I love you so."

"We've made a pretty good life for ourselves, haven't we?" Lawrence answered with sheer delight. "We may not have much for material wealth. We have a beautiful family and steady work."

Opal looked sincerely into his eyes, "Yes, we do. I think Barb and Tividar (Eva's parents) would be incredibly happy with how Eva turned out."

"Opal…." He paused and looked deep into her eyes. "We did our best," Lawrence answered, then patted her on her bottom.

She jumped and giggled at his friskiness. She lovingly took his face in her hands and kissed her lover with a tender, lingering kiss.

"All right, back to business. We have lots to do for her party before she returns. I can't believe she's eighteen. Time flies. Don't you have some art supplies to finish making for her?" Opal asked, knowing they had a lot to do before sunset.

"Yes, I've got some brushes and paint to finish making. She is going to love the new colors. I went to the meadow. Harvested some wildflowers for the base colors," Lawrence answered.

"Sounds lovely, my handsome prince. Can't wait to see them. There are scraps of butcher paper in the box under the desk that I've been saving for her to paint on too. Put those in with her gifts," Opal instructed. Mama kept working on dinner and the new apron she was making for a gift.

"Of course, my darling," Lawrence answered as he went to his woodshop to finish the gifts.

Eva ran or rode Lucy everywhere she went. She was always in a hurry. Her curiosity for life was insatiable. Today she was in a hurry to see the mayflies flit upon the rushing waters of the Tisza. They were like dancing fairies on the crests of the waves. They appeared like magic once a year during mating season.

Crowds of people from everywhere come to see the phenomenon. She tries to catch them every year and paint them. They are too fast to catch, impossible to hold still. Their lifespan is extremely short. Then the little varmints disappear in a whisp of a moment. Maybe this year will be the year to paint them perfectly, she hoped, as she was running toward her destination.

Eva began building her riverbank art studio when she was ten years old. That is when Papa and Mama finally allowed her to go by herself to the fast-flowing waters of the Tisza. It was made of sticks, stones, mud, and other natural things that she found around her chosen perfect spot. She had to rebuild a lot of it after every flood. The easel was made of long branches that were found in the nearby woods. Her brushes and paints had always been handmade of materials that she, Mama, and Papa found around home, the fields, and the butcher shop.

She carried the leather pouch full of art supplies like an old friend in her backpack. When opened, it rolled out, and each brush, made of whittled twigs and animal hair, had their own hand-sewn slot where they were safely stored. The paints had been developed over years of experimenting. The pigments were from ground herbs, flower petals, and other natural colors ground into powder and mixed with the volcanic soil that Tokaj was famous for. They were dried in the sun and made into small cakes. The water for her creations was always the fast-flowing water from the river.

After Eva lost her parents in the train accident in Budapest, painting was the most healing activity Mama and Papa found for her to do. Eva had been on that train ride with them. Searchers found her in the rubble, barely alive. Her only living relatives were her mother's parents, Mama and Papa Fallenstein. They have raised her since the accident. Her paternal grandparents were from Poland. They had passed before Eva was born. Now, at eighteen, she is tall, too thin for Mama's liking, and always on the go. The only thing she would sit still for was painting. She did take up the flute while in school, but painting is her only passion.

Eva finally stopped running when she reached the edge of the steep eight-foot bank, the entrance to her studio. She lifted the large round flat rock at the top of the bank. It was the size of a large bucket. Under the rock was the WWI waterproof ammunition box that Papa had brought back from when he served in WWI. She had noticed the box under a shelf in the butcher shop when she was five. It was empty. No one was using it. She asked Papa if she could store her paint and art supplies in it. "Of course," he said. "Yes." That was probably the best use for it. Over the years of going to the river to paint, she had it stuffed full of paint, brushes, and paper that was left over from the shop. It always kept everything dry.

After pulling the box out from under the rock, she slid down the slightly muddy bank with it under her arm. She began to set up her paints and paper. To her amazement and great surprise, she had guests in her studio, just exactly the guests that she had always hoped for, beautiful Hungarian mayflies! There was one guest that she was not so crazy about, a large ugly wolf spider and its exceptionally large web. The huge scary spider had woven its tunneled web all over the rock that she used for her chair and the easel. Its spying creepy eyes were staring at her as she set up her supplies. She could not complain. For the very first time ever, she was going to be able to paint these elusive, delicate wonders. One male and one female were caught in the web.

"You are gorgeous," she said out loud to the entangled subjects, as if they were her invited guests. There was a multitude of mayflies dancing like fairies on the river. Their wings were glistening and reflecting the rays of the sun. She was finally going to have a real chance of painting their delicate wings and pixie-like bodies that eluded her every mating season. She wanted everyone to see their beauty. If only she could capture it with her simple supplies and limited ability. What would Monet do? Her idol. She would think like Monet and give it her best effort, especially now that she has two *captive* mayflies for subjects.

The spider's web had to stay right where it was. The terrifying spider had placed it perfectly. It was skillfully attached to her easel and rock. Quickly she grabbed a few branches and put together a new easel. She spread the scraps of butcher paper across it. The artillery box served well as a chair. Reaching over to the river and dipping the paint brushes into the fast-flowing water, she was ready to begin.

The two subjects had captivated her. They jolted back and forth on the web. Her eyes were fixed on their every move. Their lifespan was relatively short. She felt awful that they were stuck there. Sometimes life leaves you stuck in a situation. Sometimes you are free.

Delicately touching the paper with angelic soft, thin strokes, hoping the wolf spider would not come out from inside its webbed tunnel. Oh, how she hated spiders. Her spine shivered just thinking about them. Hours sped by as the piece of art beautifully developed. Monet and Paris were at her fingertips. She had drifted into her dreamworld.

Chapter Two

The Spy

Music: "Jeepers Creepers" Louis Armstrong with Orchestra
"Long Gone Blues" Billie Holiday

History: January 1939 - Hitler orders Plan Z. Plan Z is a five-year naval expansion program intended to provide for a large German naval fleet proficient of defeating the Royal Navy by 1944.

This painting was achieving one of Eva's greatest accomplishments. Several hours had passed, and the mayflies were still captivating Eva's full attention. She was entranced in her subject's graceful dance and their captivity. She would set them free when she was finished with the piece. She might donate the painting to the Temple. Maybe they would hang it by the print of Monet's *Poppy Field*, the one with the lady with the umbrella and the child walking beside her. She had loved that piece since she was a child. It reminded her of her mother and her walking in the wildflowers. It completely captured her attention every time she went to Temple. It would be such an honor if they would hang her painting near it.

Eva had such concentrated tunnel vision for her painting that she did not notice the handsome young man spying on her from above. Edgar, twenty-two years old, blond hair, bright green eyes, had climbed onto the large oak branch overhanging her muddy studio. He was very curious. Snooping on this angel with long, black, tied-back hair on the bank.

Edgar was from Düsseldorf, Germany. Every summer he would visit his Uncle Prizi, Aunt Linda, and five cousins in Tokaj to work with them at their vineyard. He and his five male cousins that were like brothers to him—Samuel,

Daniel, Padraig, Peter, and Akos—had been bowhunting roebuck and hare in the woods near the river. Edgar had found a cluster of beautiful mushrooms and stopped to pick them for tonight's dinner. He had gotten distracted from his hunting party. He followed one of the deer paths down to the river where Eva was painting to see if he could find any more mushrooms. His cousins were not worried about his absence. He was known for going off by himself and catching up with them later. He did not find any more mushrooms, but he did find a breathtaking princess sitting on an old army box. He found himself completely intrigued by her sharply focused painting endeavor. He could not leave. Nothing was taking her eyes off her two light-winged subjects. Not even the sound of him climbing the old oak tree hovering over and above her with all his hunting gear.

Edgar was trying to not make a peep. He did not want to distract her from her work. He was hovering above her on what seemed to be a sturdy limb. He positioned himself to have the best bird's-eye view of this magnificent young lady below. He saw how intense she was to paint the trapped mayflies. He wiggled out a little farther to get a better view. Then, out of nowhere, the limb began to crack. The cracking became very loud, and without time to retreat from his post, he was dangling from the limb that was about to break.

His bow and quiver full of arrows fell and just about hit Eva. Eva's trance was broken, along with almost breaking her. In that instant, the limb *CRRRRAAAACKKKED!*" It fell, with Edgar holding on for dear life. Falling, as if in slow motion, nothing could stop this calamity. The limb fell on top of Edgar's right leg. Another crack was heard. It was his leg. It was broken. The limb took out Eva's painting and easel and almost her. His backpack full of mushrooms fell on top of him.

The easel, painting, and spider's web were obliterated as the limb fell on top of everything below its path. The two mayflies were untangled from the web and struggled under the debris. The female was set free. The male was crushed. The wolf spider came out and stood like a little general inspecting his quarters. He began to take the male into his possession to spin and kill him.

Eva screamed at the sight of the spider and the spy but most of all the sadness of her painting being destroyed. Tears came down her cheeks. She fell backwards into the muddy bank, paintbrush still in hand.

She sat in her bib overalls in the mud, startled, scared, and terribly upset with this stranger.

"Who are you?" she scolded him, then flung paint on him from her brush. He tried to dodge it. It went right into his eyes and ran down his cheeks. He could not dodge anything. He was stuck underneath the huge limb.

Edgar did his best to answer her and to be apologetic through his pain. "Edgar."

"Well, Edgar, you've ruined my painting that I have waited years to paint. I finally had the perfect setup to paint them," Eva grumbled and snarled at him.

"I am so sorry," Edgar answered in a mumble, while turning pale.

"Oh, my gosh, you are hurt so badly," Eva said with compassion, turning her attention to the more urgent matter.

"Yeah, I was hoping you'd notice," he said with a bit of sarcasm as he was trying to not pass out. "I think my leg is broken," Edgar said, while gasping with pain. "Can you go to the Schwartzes' vineyard? Get my uncle and aunt. Do you know where that is?"

"Yes, of course. Everyone knows where the Schwartz vineyard is," Eva said with surprise.

She had never been there. Everyone in the valley knew of the famous Schwartz Vineyard. It is the foremost vineyard in the region. The most highly prized wines come from this vineyard. The Schwartzes are a large, hard-working Jewish family. The kitchen help would come to the butcher shop several times a month to pick up large orders. Eva had never actually met any of the Schwartzes. But of course, she knew who they were and where their farm and vineyard were located.

Eva steadied Edgar very securely in a comfortable position so that he would not fall. Then she smacked him lightly on the head with her paintbrush.

"That's for ruining my painting," Eva said with the strange mixture of sarcasm, justice, and an ornery smile. "I'll be right back. Don't move," Eva instructed.

"I don't think I can," Edgar said smugly under his breath with the usual wit that he was known for. He was getting light-headed. He did not mention it. He did not want to scare her. The limb was too heavy for the two of them to move. Besides that, the pressure from it was helping to stop the bleeding. Eva had to move fast to keep him from bleeding out. She ran through the woods faster than she had ever run before.

Chapter Three

Run for Help

Music: "If I Didn't Care" The Ink Spots

"Flying Home" Benny Goodman Sextet with Charlie Christian and Lionel Hampton

History: March 14 The pro-German Slovak Republic is created. Carpatho-Ukraine is created, which Hungary invades that same day.

Eva tore through the woods heading east on the deer path toward the Schwartzes' estate, running as fast as she could in her black, leather work boots. It would be dusk soon. She knew he needed medical attention quickly. She did not forget the promise that she had made to Mama about being home for supper and Shabbat. She had to do the right thing for this young man. Mama and Papa would understand. She knew they would be worried. She had to reach the Schwartzes as quickly as possible.

The deer path led to the back of the estate. There was a large wrought iron gate at the back entrance. An eight-foot stone wall surrounded the mansion and barns. The gate was locked. It was taller than the stone fortress by about a foot. It was heavy iron with spikes at the top for decoration and security. Eva yelled as loudly as she could to get someone's attention. No one could hear her over the loud steam thresher and farm machinery being repaired at the barnyard. She decided she had to climb the gate, hoping they did not have any large dogs that would come after her as she threw herself over to the other side.

Up she went with her skinny, but strong, arms and legs. She was just about over the sharp iron spikes at the top when her thick leather work boots got stuck in between the iron spikes at the top of the gate. She flipped herself over the spikes and was hanging upside down with her right foot caught in the spikes on the top of the gate. One of the spikes sliced through and caught her bib overall straps, causing her to dangle helplessly upside down and sway back and forth on the gate. Her long coal black hair waving in the breeze.

Her screaming for help was going unnoticed for what seemed an eternity. It was about ten minutes. Finally, one of the farmhands, the oldest one, Sandor, noticed something out of the corner of his eye while he was working on the thresher. He stopped the engine and the work and told Edgar's five cousins to run and help this dangling girl at the gate. Four of the boys and Sandor jumped on the hay wagon. It was already hooked up to the tractor. Samuel, the oldest cousin, drove the tractor and wagon down the dirt lane as fast as he could. None of them could imagine who this crazy person was hanging on their gate. They were so shocked they did not know whether to laugh or to be terrified. Mostly they were laughing. Why was this silly person trying to get into their vineyard by the back gate when the front gate is wide open?

Eva saw the tractor and wagon racing down the lane toward her. She was so thankful to see someone coming that tears came to her eyes. She had screamed so long and so loud in her precarious upside-down state that her throat was dry. She could barely speak. Samuel drove the tractor beside the gate and lined up the wagon underneath her. Sandor and the boys were trying to not laugh as they helped this dirty, paint-covered, disheveled, attractive girl down from the ornate spikes of their gate.

"What the hell?" asked Samuel, the oldest cousin.

Eva cleared her throat and could only utter one word. "Edgar."

"Edgar?" they all repeated with fear.

The entire tone of the moment changed when she uttered his name.

"Where is he, miss?" asked Sandor, with a demanding voice.

She cleared her throat and spoke as best she could, "River." She coughed and pointed to the deer path that she just came from.

Sandor, who was like an uncle to the boys, gave her a drink of water from his old army canteen that he always kept on the tractor.

The cousins opened the gate and asked if she was strong enough to take them there. She was. She nodded, "Yes."

"You boys go find him," Sandor directed. "I'll go get your parents. Is he right on the riverbank?"

"Yes, about a mile from here," Eva answered, getting her voice back. "He's hurt. I think his leg is broken in more than one place."

Sandor threw her his canteen and motioned for all of them to run as fast as they could.

The boys quickly followed her through the woods. They could hardly keep up with her pace. They were strong, fit boys, but she was like a cheetah running through the well-worn paths. Time was of the essence. It was getting dark.

Meanwhile, Mama and Papa were worried about Eva. She should have been home by now. They hurried down to the river's edge to find her. They found Edgar and heard the entire story. He was weak but in good humor. They laughed when he told them Eva had thrown paint at him and thumped him on the head with her paintbrush.

"Well, you did deserve it," said Mama.

Edgar smiled and nodded in agreement.

"That sounds like Eva. She can be a little hot-tempered, even though you did deserve it," Papa said, as he wrapped a long, straight stick he had found around Edgar's leg to keep it secured until the Schwartzes arrived.

It looked as if it was a compound fracture of the tibia. Papa had been a medic in WWI. His field dressing experience came back to him immediately. Opal was impressed. She had hardly heard him speak of his war experiences. To see him in action was admirable. They kept their patient stable and alert as possible until help arrived.

Eva and the cousins came tearing through the woods. They slid down the bank and began working to get Edgar ready for transport. Eva was so glad to see Mama and Papa. She knew Edgar was in good hands when she saw they were there. Sandor, Uncle Prizi, and Aunt Linda decided to bring the motorboat down to the bank. It would be the fastest way to get him to their doctor. They arrived soon after Eva and the boys got there. Edgar was pale, speaking to them, but going into shock and in and out of consciousness. Mama and Papa had kept him safe. The cousins took off their shirts and tied them to two long branches. They made a makeshift stretcher.

Aunt Linda, Uncle Prizi, and Sandor jumped out of the boat and onto the shore. The boys, Lawrence, Opal, and Eva had removed the large broken limb away from Edgar and gingerly placed him onto the stretcher. They passed him over to Sandor, Prizi, and Linda, who then carried him over the muddy bank and flowing water onto the boat. They wasted no time. He had lost blood. They did not know how much. They sped off as fast as they could. The doctor's house was upriver on the other side of the river in Tokaj.

The doctor happened to be out on his dock cleaning the fish he had caught. He saw them coming. He recognized them and their boat. He put down his fillet knife and ran out to meet them at the river's edge. Aunt Linda gave Dr. Nargy as much information as she could regarding Edgar's condition. The men carried Edgar to the doctor's kitchen and laid him on the table. The doctor set his leg for transport to the hospital. It was his tibia that was broken, possibly his fibula. He hoped the knee was untouched by the accident. The tibia had broken through his skin. He would have to go to the surgeon at the hospital immediately. X-rays will be needed. The doctor drove them to the hospital. Linda and Prizi were holding Edgar on their laps in the back of the doctor's van. Sandor headed back to the vineyard with the boat. It took Edgar three days under doctor's care before he would be able to come back home.

Back at the riverbank at Eva's torn-up painting area, Edgar's cousins—Samuel, seventeen; Daniel, sixteen; twins Peter and Padraig, eleven; and Akos, eight years old—helped her clean up the mess. The boys reassured Opal and Lawrence that they will walk her home when they got done. Mama and Papa walked home knowing that she is in good hands. She tucked her painting supplies back into the WWI box and placed it under the big rock. The cousins walked her home as promised. They invited her and her grandparents to the vineyard. They politely declined at this time. They would love to come over in the future.

"Thank you very much for walking me home. We'll be staying home tonight. It's Shabbat and my birthday," Eva explained further.

All the cousins chimed in and wished her a happy birthday.

"Thank you so much," Eva responded gratefully.

"I'm sure Mother and Father will want you all to come over for a meal soon. To thank you for helping Edgar," Samuel invited. "We'll figure out a date that is good for all of us."

"Thank you," Papa and Mama said, shaking each of the boys' hands.

The boys departed from their new friends and walked back home.

Shabbat was peacefully held in both homes that evening.

The goulash and Dobos cake were eaten for Eva's birthday.

Eva turned eighteen without a painting of her most anticipated subjects. She met an entire new family of friends. Met an interesting young man to ponder. Went to bed hoping he would be all right, still mad at him for ruining her painting.

Chapter Four

Rocky and the Neighborly Invite

Music: Beer Barrel Polka (Roll Out the Barrel) Will Glahe & his Orchestra "Back in the Saddle Again" Gene Autry

History: March 15 Germany occupies Bohemia and Moravia-Silesia. This was in violation of the Munich Agreement. The Czechs do not put up any organized resistance, having lost their main defensive line with the annexation of the Sudetenland. Germany establishes the Protectorate of Bohemia and Moravia.

Three days later, early afternoon, Eva, Mama, and Papa were working at the butcher shop. There were many orders to be filled preparing for Tuesday, delivery day.

From the large window in the front of the shop they could see a stunning, almost royal-looking, horse and rider coming down the road toward the shop. They stopped their work and ran to the window to see who this was. The very tall, probably sixteen hands, glistening black draft horse was trotting toward their shop. Papa knew it was a Nonius breed from its gait. Not too many people around this area could afford this breed. The magnificent horse was decked out with a beautiful ornamental saddle and reins.

The long, luscious, flowing mane was show quality. The rider sat perfectly straight in the unique ornate saddle. When the rider came into view, they realized it was a lady. She was wearing long black leather boots and jodhpurs. Usually, ladies would ride sidesaddle. She was not riding sidesaddle. They had never seen this before. Her jacket was long and fitted. The horse was huge, stout, and perfectly groomed, a nobleman's breed, highly prized.

Papa opened the door. They all walked out. The three of them gawked at its oncoming dazzling presence. They tried to not be seen gawking. Its muscular body and stride, *clip clop*, *clip clop*, up the cobblestone street. They could not help themselves. They were gawking. Who could it be? They had never seen any horse or rider like this come to their little shop.

All the work in the shop had come to a stop. Their eyes were fixed on what appeared to be something out of the movies. The rider was tying the horse up to the tree across the road. All they could see was her back, her long brown hair and slender athletic build. Her beautiful riding outfit looked like a member of the royal family had shown up at their shop.

The rider turned to come toward the shop. They all cleared their throats and backed back into the shop and away from the door. They were trying to act like they had not been staring at her and her horse.

The beautiful, tall, model-type lady walked through the door. The bell on the top of the door rang. She said with a sweet voice, "Hello, is Eva here?"

Eva looked at Mama and Papa, and she shrugged her shoulders. She had no idea who this lady is. None of them recognized her.

"I'm Eva," she answered courteously.

"I'm Linda Schwartz. I came to thank you for saving my nephew, Edgar."

None of them had recognized her from the other night. It was dusk and all their focus was on Edgar.

"Oh, my goodness, well, you're welcome," Eva said, feeling a little guilty for throwing paint on him and smacking him on the head after he ruined her painting, hoping he did not mention that to his Aunt.

"My husband Prizi and I would like to invite all of you to dinner in a couple of days, if that works for you. I usually send our cook to buy meat from you. This time I needed to meet the lovely lady and your family that courageously saved Edgar. He is home now. He will be in a wheelchair for a while. His tibia and fibula are broken. Luckily, his knee was not hurt. There was some blood loss. But, thanks to your care, he survived the accident very well. He'll be in a cast for a couple of months, if all goes well. We've hired a nurse to help him. We would like to thank you for helping him," Linda explained and invited.

Eva looked at Papa and Mama for permission. The invitation was wholeheartedly accepted.

"Thank you. We would love to," answered Papa. "I'm Lawrence. This is my wife, Opal." He accepted and shook Linda's hand.

"What can we bring?" asked Opal.

"You can bring dessert," Linda answered. "We've heard of your famous desserts from our cooks."

Mama blushed. She did not know she had a reputation.

"We'll order twenty-five pounds of your best meats for grilling. You know what we like. A mix of your best grilling meats. I've got a lot of hungry boys to feed. We'll have some of the pheasants and partridges that they shot on their hunts too. I'll send my cooks to pick up the order late tomorrow. We'd like to treat you to an evening of entertainment, food, and our specialty wines for helping Edgar. Does six o'clock sound good for you?" Linda invited.

Papa and Mama accepted with handshakes and smiles.

Eva said, "Thank you." She could not keep her eyes off the elegant horse. She kept peering conspicuously out the window at him. She was trying to not be rude to their guest. Linda understood Eva's overwhelming interest in her horse. Eva reminded her of herself when she was that age.

"Would you like to ride him?" Linda asked.

"Me? Ride him?" Eva was shocked that she would invite her to ride this marvelous stallion.

He was the tallest horse she had ever seen. She was used to riding Lucy bareback through the mountain paths. She never knew what it was like to ride a stallion that was perfectly groomed, as if for show, with tack that looked like only majestic families would own.

"Do you think I could?" she asked Linda and at the same time looked back at Mama and Papa for permission.

They both nodded yes, knowing she could handle him.

"Yes, of course. How much experience do you have riding?" Linda asked.

"I ride our delivery horse, Lucy, bareback," answered Eva with a bit of embarrassment.

"You'll do great. Bareback is how I started as a young girl. Rocky is his name. He's fully broken," Linda encouraged. "Come on out and climb up on him. He's very gentle. He listens well."

Eva took her apron off. She had her usual bib overalls and work boots on. She took a string from the butcher shop counter and tied her hair back into a ponytail.

Eva did not want to appear scared or weak. Animals can read that. She walked up to Rocky's broad muscular neck and petted his silky, perfectly groomed black coat and mane, talked with him, looked him in the eyes until they had an understanding, let him get to know her, then hoisted herself up on the saddle like she had done it her entire life. She had never sat in such a lovely ornate saddle. Most ladies were still using sidesaddles. Linda seemed so sophisticated and modern. Eva sat firmly on the horse using her whole body to talk with him, her thighs and calves locked on to his wide strong body. She felt his muscles. He felt her confidence. The language of communication was instant between them. He responded like a dream.

Eva looked back to check to see how Mama, Papa, and Linda were reacting to her riding away down the cobblestone street. *Clippity clop, Clippity clop*, the thunderous sound of his wide-shoed hooves was musical. Rocky began to move faster under her command, strong and steady down the narrow street. Mama, Papa, and Linda watched as she waved to the people and especially the little children walking on the sidewalks. She knew each of them. They were neighbors and customers. Everyone stopped and waved as Eva's long black ponytail was flying in the wind while riding the most beautiful horse that had been in town in an exceptionally long time. After about seven blocks of riding Rocky, she turned around and trotted him back to Linda. His gait was brilliant and powerful. Not like a racehorse. Like a robust tank that could go forever.

Eva wanted to continue riding. She did not want to be rude. She sat straight up in the saddle like she owned him as she rode him back to Linda. She thanked Linda profusely for allowing her to ride such a magnificent beast. Eva climbed down from his tall stance and wide powerful back. She thanked Rocky by patting his neck. He curled his large stout head back to her and nuzzled her with his nose. She was amazed at his strength and his tenderness.

"You have trained and loved Rocky so much. It shows," Eva complimented Linda as she handed back the reins.

"We've had him since he was a foal. He's eight now. He may be a huge giant of a horse. But he's just our big, spoiled baby. If you would like to ride him or any of our horses, you are more than welcome to come learn about them and ride them, anytime," Linda offered, knowing that Edgar would like to see more of her too.

Eva smiled a huge, ear-to-ear smile. Mama and Papa, nodded to her simultaneously knowing that she would leap at that opportunity.

She looked to them for approval of the generous offer. They gave her the okay with a nod and smiles. They liked the idea of Eva getting to know Edgar a little better too.

Eva answered Linda excitedly, "I would love to." She was willing to come ride and learn everything about her horses.

"Of course, you know that means mucking out their stalls too?" Linda said with a smile and a wink.

Papa, Mama, and Eva laughed in agreement.

"Not a problem there," Eva laughed. "I have mucked out many stalls."

Linda mounted Rocky and bid them all a very loving, neighborly goodbye. "I'll send my cooks to pick up the meat late tomorrow. See you in a couple days."

She rode off with a smile and a wave on the gallant horse. Eva felt like she had just met a lifelong friend. She was amazed at her kindness and strength.

Linda could tell Eva would be good with horses. She had a gentle understanding spirit and strength about her. She would like to encourage that. She never had a daughter. She would love to take her under her wing. She also thought it would be good if she and Edgar spent some time together. Mama seemed to pick up on that too.

Edgar had not stopped asking Aunt Linda about his "angel" by the river. His cousins were about sick of hearing about her. They, as brothers or close cousins do, teased him relentlessly every time he brought up her name.

Papa, Mama, and Eva began to prepare for the large order that Linda gave them.

"What dessert will you be making for the dinner?" Eva asked Mama.

"Oh, I don't know, I thought maybe you could make a dessert this time. It might impress Edgar to see that you can cook," Mama said.

Papa chuckled knowing that Opal and Linda had somehow connected on a motherly level that did not need words to communicate.

"What? Wait, what?" Eva asked, surprised at Mama's answer. "But I can't bake like you can. I don't think my cooking would impress anyone. Besides that, I don't want to impress anyone." Eva was almost stuttering at the thought of impressing anyone with her cooking, especially a boy that ruined her painting. All she ever wanted to do was go to Paris and become a painter like Monet. She was not interested in any boys around here.

"You're cooking up something more than dessert here, Mama," Eva stated, a bit confused at the notion of a sneaky plot.

"Am I?" Mama smiled slyly back.

Papa just laughed and left the room. He thought it safer that way.

Chapter Five

The Dinner

Music: "Three Little Fishies" Kay Kiser
"Jumpin' Jive" Cab Calloway & His Cotton Club Orchestra
History: March 16 - Hungary annexes the Carpatho-Ukraine.

Papa was at the barn getting Lucy and the delivery cart hitched for the ride over to the Schwartzes. The cart had been handed down to Papa from his father who had started the butcher shop with his father. It had four large, wooden spoke wheels that Papa was always repairing to keep the cart ready to deliver through the rough mountains and valley roads around Tokaj. Papa had painted it bright yellow with white trim and black lettering on each side that said Fallenstein's Butcher Shop. Everyone knew it was Papa coming on delivery days. They could not miss the bright yellow delivery wagon from far away. That is why he chose that color. Everyone knew when he was making deliveries. The buckboard was just wide enough to hold the three of them. Mama sat in the middle. Eva would help Mama on and off the buckboard. It was tall, and Mama was a short and a pleasingly plump woman. Eva was taller than both of them. She had gotten her height from her father.

Eva was in her bedroom getting dressed. She thought she would wear her bib overalls in case she got to ride Rocky or any of the horses or if she got to work with them in the barn or even muck out a stall. All she could think of was Rocky.

Mama passed by her room and saw what she was wearing. "No, No, baby," Mama scolded. Shook her head. Put her hands on her hips. Eva knew what that meant. Mama stood at Eva's bedroom door and was not letting up on that cold, hard, motherly stare for anything.

"What do you mean?" Eva said honestly bewildered.

"You can't wear bib overalls to a nice dinner," Mama said.

"I know it's usually not what we would wear." She hesitated and looked at herself in the tiny mirror on the wall, "I think Linda will let me ride Rocky," Eva said with hopefulness.

"I see." Mama shook her head. "All you are thinking of is the horse. You're not thinking of the boy? Edgar?"

"No," Eva said with a shock. "Why would I? He's the rudest human being I've ever met."

"Hmph," Mama said with a little giggle. "I think Linda wants you to think of Edgar more than Rocky. I saw it in her eyes. She told me he can't stop talking about you."

"What? When did she say that?" Eva asked.

"When you were riding Rocky up the street," Mama answered. "She said his cousins were teasing him profusely because he wouldn't stop talking about you. Sounds like he's sweet on you."

"Sounds like he's lost his mind. I'm definitely going to wear the overalls. I'm not interested in him. He was so rude that day. I was almost done with my painting. He was spying on me. That was creepy. He ruined my painting and ruined my day." Eva stomped her foot and folded her arms in defiance.

"I'm sure he'll make up for it." Mama reassured her with a bit of a sneaky voice.

"Ha, unlikely. I waited forever to paint those mayflies. There were two caught in a spider's web. I was almost done with my painting. He fell on it and ruined it. Serves him right for getting a broken leg. "Eva said with a mean tone."

"Now, Eva, that's not very nice," Mama laughed.

"Well, no, it's not, but he really made me mad. I flung paint on him and hit him on the head with my paintbrush." Eva laughed at herself for being rude too. "I guess I was rude too. I'll be on my best behavior. I finished making the kolache cookies too. I didn't find the apricot filling we had put up last year. I used lekvar."

"Well, I guess he's lucky he didn't get a concussion too." Mama smiled. "Yes, I smelled them earlier. They will love them. Now, go put on your white cotton sundress and tie your hair back. That young man thought you looked pretty in bib overalls. He is going to really see how beautiful you are when you clean up. Just try not to fling anything at him or hit him this time." Mama smiled and shook her head at her.

"All right," Eva laughed. "But I'm bringing my bib overalls along, just in case Linda invites me to ride Rocky."

"Yes, baby." Mama rolled her eyes and left to get dressed in her best.

Papa calls out from the barn to let the ladies know that he and Lucy are ready to go. Mama is bringing her famous cinnamon streusel cake to share with the dinner party. It is still warm and the smell is filling up the house.

Eva comes out of her tiny bedroom with her white sundress on. Mama had made it for her last summer. She did not realize how tall Eva had gotten. The dress was a little more snug around the breasts and a little shorter than she realized it would be. Eva shrugged not knowing what to do. She had not been in this dress in so long. She did not realize she had that much bigger breasts either.

"Guess these things just creep up on ya?" Eva said with a curl of her lip and a curious smile.

"For goodness' sake. Let me see if I have something you can wear." Mama said in a bit of a panic.

"I don't think I could fit anything of yours, Mama." Eva said, hoping she could go back to her bibs.

Eva and Mama knew that there was nothing in Mama's wardrobe that would be fitting for a young girl. Plus, Mama was about a foot shorter than Eva and about a foot wider.

"Go next door. Borrow a dress from Helena," Mama instructed.

Helena had been Eva's best friend since they were little. Mama shooed her out the door with both hands.

"Ok, I'll be right back." Eva answered as she ran out the front door.

About ten minutes later, Eva came rushing back with a suitable pink summer dress. Helena was a little bigger in the top than Eva. It was a little baggy, but at least it wasn't from the last century, like Mama's clothes. It was not too tight or too short. It would do.

"That will work," Mama said with relief.

A heavy rain had passed through the valley earlier in the day. It left the dirt roads muddy with puddles all the way over to the vineyard.

Papa sat on the left side of the buckboard, holding Lucy's reins. He reached over the buckboard and pulled Mama up as Eva was helping her from behind. The mud from Mama's shoes had splashed up into the carriage and had splattered Helena's pink dress. Eva did not mind. It would wash out. Mama felt bad about it. She wanted this to be a beautiful evening showing off their beautiful Eva to their wonderful neighbors. Down the road they trotted. They turned the last corner, almost to the vineyard, Mama's large straw sun hat got caught by the wind and flew off her head. It landed in a large murky mud puddle on the side of the road. Papa halted Lucy. Eva looked at Mama with a "really?" kind of look. She knew she was going to be the one to go get it. She was muddy enough already. Mama could only look into her eyes and ask forgiveness with her puppy dog eyes and shrug her shoulders.

Eva jumped down to retrieve the sun hat. Mud splattered. Shook her head in disbelief. Tossed it in the back of the delivery wagon and laughed at herself and how muddy she had become on the ride over.

"Well, good thing I brought my bib overalls." Eva said as she hopped back up on the buckboard.

Papa drove on with a grin, shaking his head in disbelief. Eva and Mama just laughed at themselves.

"We tried," said Mama "They'll just have to understand. We're country folks. Hope they are too."

Clippity clop, clippity clop, Lucy made her way passed the large stone wall at the vineyard property. Then turned to go through the large ornate iron front gate with the huge "S" in the middle of it.

Eva and Mama were stunned at the beauty of the stone mansion that was down the long, oak tree-lined lane. It looked almost like a castle. Papa was astonished at the barns that were behind the mansion. They had heard of the beauty of this vineyard. They had never been through the front gates. They had always heard of the family that lived here. The five boys were ages eight to seventeen. They were known to be a raucous bunch of boys but also known to be hard workers. Mama had also heard that they loved music. Each of the boys knew how to play instruments. Eva played the flute. Mama had made her bring it in case there was a chance she could play after supper. Mama and Papa loved singing and dancing. They were adorable when they danced around the house. He towered over Mama and was thin. Eva loved watching them do some folk dancing when they were not too tired from work. They had not had a chance to do much of that in a long time. Seems like they were always working. Or too tired to do it after working so much.

As they approached the large horseshoe shaped driveway in front of the main entrance, the head farmhand, Sandor, was at the entrance of the grand portico of the main house. Eva recognized him from the day Edgar was hurt. They did not know it at the time but it was strange that the farmhand would be greeting them. He apologized that the Mr. and Mrs. of the house were not there to greet them. They had been out back trying to get the horses back to the barn earlier just after the rain, and they had fallen in the mud. Eva and Mama drew a huge sigh of relief. They were country people, just like them. They will understand the mud splashed on the bright yellow delivery truck, Lucy, and Eva's pink dress.

Sandor assisted the ladies down and helped them to the front entrance of the house. They sat in the parlor until Linda came to greet them.

After getting the ladies settled in, Sandor jumped up onto the buckboard and directed Lawrence to the barn. They unhitched Lucy, groomed her, put her in a beautiful clean stall where she could eat, drink, and rest until dinner was over. They hosed the mud off the cart. Papa and Sandor hit it off very well. They discovered that they had both served in WWI in different regiments. When their work was done at the barn, they went to the house for drinks, dinner, and more conversation.

Linda and her husband, Prizi, came down the long exquisite central staircase in the two-story stately foyer. The parlor was located to the west of the foyer through its grand arched entrance. They had both tidied up. They looked festive but comfortable. Opal and Eva were happy they were down to earth. They felt very relaxed to be with them. The house became a home. They made it very inviting to be there. Linda was in a simple cotton flower print dress and flat shoes. Prizi was in black dress pants with a bright white shirt, dark green vest with silver-colored buttons. Linda's long flowing chestnut colored hair draped over her shoulders. Her smile was warm and inviting. Prizi had thick black hair and strong jaw line. He looked as if he could be a military man. He held himself with shoulders back with a military stride. They were both tan from working outside in the vineyard. They were a beautiful happy couple. Eva and Mama were glued to the sight of them. They did not mean to stare. They could not help themselves. Their beauty was striking.

"Hello, Eva and Opal," Linda said as she took her last step off the grand staircase. "This is Prizi, my husband. Sorry we weren't there to greet you. Did Sandor tell you, we both fell out in the barnyard in the mud and muck, trying to get the horses up to their stalls?"

Mama and Eva tried to hold back their giggles. They could not.

"I know, it was a funny sight," Prizi said.

"No, it's not that. "It's that I too fell in the mud on the way over, and this is a borrowed dress because the only dress I had was too small. I hadn't worn it since last year. Then Mama's hat flew off in the breeze on the way over, and it was too late to turn back. We were afraid you wouldn't understand my dress being muddy." Eva said with a dispensation of words that flew so fast it made Linda and Prizi adore her honesty and goodness.

They all laughed.

"Oh, honey, we live with mud and worse, all the time. We're not fancy people. We're farmers. If we don't come home with dirt or mud on us, something is very wrong," Linda explained.

"Would you like to clean up upstairs? I can see if I can find you one of my dresses to wear?" Linda offered.

"Really?" Eva said excitedly, "I did bring my work clothes if you needed any help with Rocky or mucking stalls."

"You are just like me," Linda said giving her a hug, "Let's get you upstairs before all the festivities begin. I would love to share a dress with you. I have five boys, Edgar makes six in the summer, and a husband. I never get to have any girl time. Let's go upstairs and pick out a pretty dress for you."

Eva looks back at Mama with a huge smile, then dashes up the stairs with Linda. She brings her bib overalls with her and hopes that she can change into them later to go to the barns.

Mama is escorted graciously to the terrace by Prizi. He offers her his elbow. She takes it delicately and feels like a queen escorted by a handsome prince. She could get used to this. They reach Lawrence and Sandor at the table where they are already engaged in laughter and drinks and cigars. You would have thought they had known each other for a lifetime. They were like two old friends catching up on old times. Lawrence introduced Opal to Sandor. Sandor introduced Prizi to Lawrence.

"Would you like to try some of our finest wines, Madam?" Sandor offers.

"Yes, please," Opal answered with great anticipation. Everyone knew about how wonderful the Schwartzes' wines were. The Azur was a fine wine which had been produced for kings for centuries.

Sandor went to the wine table and poured everyone a round of the vineyard's oldest, most treasured wine. Opal and Lawrence felt very well taken care of by their hosts. Lawrence offered a very loving, respectful toast to their hosts.

The stone terrace's thick oak trellises are heavy laden with wisteria dripping from every ledge. The tables were set exquisitely with white linen and their best china. The cooks were grilling on the massive outdoor grills.

The aroma was intoxicating. Wine was being poured by the kitchen staff as soon as their glasses were empty. They brought out their best wines from many years vintage, including Azur. Azur was so rich that it was served in small portions in specially made ornate teaspoons.

Music was on its way. The boys marched onto the terrace with their instruments in hand. Samuel on guitar. Daniel carrying his violin. Peter with the large double bass. Padraig on the zither. Akos on the violin, or fiddle, as he preferred to call it. Prizi can play the Duda and violin, especially when he has drunk enough. Linda plays the violin. The Schwartzes loved to entertain and party. The boys were marching onto the terrace with confidence. Ready to entertain their guests. Edgar was being pushed in his wheelchair by his nurse, Dahlia, at the end of the line of young men that he considered brothers.

Like a military commander, Prizi stopped the parade of young men in their tracks to introduce them to Lawrence and Opal. Sandor, of course, knew them all since they were born. Sandor had worked at the vineyard since he was a young boy. He was a teenager when Prizi's father hired him. He watched Prizi grow up. Prizi's sons were like nephews to him and his wife Rita. Rita was over the work in the kitchen. They lived in a small cabin on the vineyard.

The boys were dressed in black pants, bright white, pressed, starched shirts, different colored vests with silver buttons, similar to what their Father was wearing. They had black hair, cut short, like a military cut. Edgar had blonde hair. He took after his father.

The musicians for the evening politely excused themselves after being introduced to Opal and Lawrence. They went to the sunny side of the terrace to set up to play some folk music before dinner. The boys asked where Linda and Eva were. Edgar was especially craning his neck to see where Eva might be. The boys were making fun of him already, and the evening was young.

Prizi told them about the mud situation. Then explained that Linda was helping Eva find another dress to wear.

Edgar turned red on her account. He thought to himself how embarrassing that must have been for her.

Opal, Lawrence, Sandor, and Prizi sat down again at one of the finely adorned, ten-foot dining tables, enjoying the exquisite wine and wonderful conversation. The music began. Toes started tapping. The aroma of the barbecue was in the air. The massive amount and variety of meat was sizzling on the enormous stone grills. There were two chefs at the grills, and three waitresses serving drinks and hors d'oeuvres.

The cousins were playing traditional Hungarian folk music. Opal noticed that Edgar's playing was different. He was not playing a violin. She assumed it was a violin by the case that had been on his lap. It was a viola. The deep lower tones of the viola were gripping Mama's heart. When he played it, it was like he sunk his entire soul into the piece. His fingers were dancing on the strings like a hummingbird's wings. It was as if the instrument was one with him, an extension of his heart. His eyes were closed most of the time. He was lost in the tones, as if he were in a supernatural reverie. It was precise and polished. She had never seen or heard anything like it before. Her heart was melting with the power of his playing. While the men were talking farming and politics, she could not take her eyes off this gripping musician. The other boys were good. They tended to be rough and rowdy with their instruments. They were folksy and played hard, not powerful and yet tender like Edgar. He was just as big and muscular as the rest of the boys, from working on the farm. There was a spiritual connection he had with the viola. Mama was mesmerized by him and his playing. She could not wait for Eva to hear him.

Lawrence, Sandor, and Prizi were drinking more and more. The conversation between them was getting political and heated. Lawrence and Sandor disagreed with Hungary joining the Axis powers with Germany. They were more nationalists. Lawrence and Sandor's experiences in WWI gave them a different perspective than Prizi. They had seen war first-hand. Prizi was younger. He had never seen war firsthand. Prizi liked the improvement in the economy while being in alliance with Germany. Hungary had been in such a deep depression that they sought the Axis powers alignment to help get out of it. The more the three of them drank, the more heated the conversation became. Opal was worried about how heated their conversation was becoming.

Lawrence and Sandor disagreed firmly with Prizi. They did not trust Germany and the direction it was headed. Opal was trying to ignore their conversation and listen to the music. Then out of nowhere a fist slammed down on the table. Slammed down so hard that it knocked some of the glasses off the table and broke one. Startled, Opal looked behind her. Sandor was standing up with the fist still on the table.

"Sit down, Sandor," Prizi demanded, "You know we don't agree on these matters."

"We never will," Sandor said with a fury, "If your Father were still alive, he'd set you straight."

"Well, I guess that's your job now, Sandor," Prizi said with respect for his old friend, "We may not agree on these political matters, but I will always love you."

Prizi reached across the table and gently put his hand on Sandor's fist. Sandor sat down and realized Prizi was not the problem. Germany's politics were the problem.

"I love you too, Prizi. No matter how stubborn you may be," Sandor said with a heartfelt apology.

Opal gave Papa that "look" that told him to "shhh." She wanted to hear the beautiful folk music that the boys were playing. Papa agreed. He did not want to get into a heated fight over politics on their first visit.

Suddenly, Edgar stopped playing his viola. Mama's concentration was interrupted by the abrupt stop of his playing. The other boys stopped playing too. The expressions on their faces were awe and mesmerized. All their jaws dropped.

Mama saw all the boys staring at the entrance of the terrace. They could see the grand foyer and central staircase from there. It was Eva and Linda. Really… it was Eva. She was stunning. Linda had fixed her hair. Put a touch of rouge and lipstick on her captivating full lips and high cheek bones. Mama and Papa's jaws dropped too.

No wonder it was taking them a little while to get downstairs. She did not just throw on a dress. Linda gave her a makeover. Although, she did not need much. Her natural beauty shows through no matter what she is wearing.

Linda had applied just enough make-up to give her a hint of color. Her long, glistening, coal black, wavy hair was put up with a sophisticated soft bun. There were a few strands of hair perfectly placed to frame her face. She looked like a goddess. At least that is what Edgar thought. The elegant light blue silk, sleeveless dress draped over her like a lovely ballerina. The dainty black ballerina type shoes fit her perfectly. She stepped onto the terrace like divinity and took everyone's breath away.

All of the boys' jaws were still dangling wide open. They would never again tease Edgar about his "river angel." Edgar just sighed with relief to see her. He puffed out his chest to the cousins to let them all know that he knew how precious she was the whole time. He knew from the moment he saw her that she was an angel that had come to earth.

"Look, the musicians are ready to play," said Linda, trying to stop the boys from awkwardly gawking so Eva would not feel funny as she walked with a natural elegance to the table.

Eva was unaware she was turning heads. She was so happy to be hanging out with her newfound friend, Linda. She was like a big sister. They could not stop talking about horses, make-up, art, painting. They were both ecstatic with their newfound bond.

Papa and Mama had never seen their baby with makeup on. It made them gush and stare at her too. She was not their little girl anymore. She was grown up. She was stunning. She had breasts. When did that happen? They both realized that at the same time. They teared up and looked at each other in agreement, without saying a word. They watched her elegantly stroll onto the terrace with Linda. They knew she had no idea the impression she was making on everyone. It all came so natural for her.

Edgar was spellbound. He put his viola on his lap, almost dropping it. He could not take his eyes off her. He knew this was going to be the young lady he would marry. He also smirked to himself knowing that now his cousins were seeing what he had seen from the very first moment he saw her painting on the bank of the Tisza.

"Eva, come over here and sit by your grandparents," Linda guided, "I'll get you a drink of our finest wines. If it's okay with your grandparents?" Linda asked as she looked to Opal and Lawrence for approval.

Papa nodded, "Yes." He was realizing, in that moment, that she was a young lady. Somehow he had been thinking of her as his little girl still. He felt himself tearing up. Mama had tears welling up too. She caught herself and elbowed Papa, so that they did not make a scene for Eva.

"I'll pour a little white wine for you before dinner." Linda explained while pouring more wine in everyone's glasses. "We'll try the red during dinner, with the beautiful meat from your shop, and after dinner I want all of you to try our Azur."

Mama and Papa could never afford a bottle of Azur. They were very thankful to try some of these luscious wines from the best winemakers.

"Listen to the boys play some of their favorite music. I think you'll like it." Linda invited everyone. "Feel free to dance if you'd like."

Eva looked over at the boys. They looked different than she remembered when she had seen them a few days ago. For one thing, they were clean and dressed up. They were as raucous as she remembered though. However, Edgar was different than his cousins. Edgar's eyes looked extremely inviting. He sat leaning forward a little, wanting to get up. Of course, he could not because of his broken leg. It was outstretched, elevated for better circulation. Dahlia, his nurse, standing by if he needed anything. He hated that he could not get up and dance with Eva.

The boys began to play some traditional Hungarian folk songs again. Mama was tapping her toes. Papa was listening to the music. He was also engaged, thanks to the increased drinking, in the ever-more-intensely, growing conversation of politics with Prizi and Sandor again. The more they drank, the louder they were getting again. Rita came out of the kitchen and grabbed Sandor to pull him away from the heated political discussion. Mama followed her lead. She grabbed Papa to dance with her. Linda nudged Prizi to give Eva a whirl on the dance floor. Eva gladly got up and danced. She loved dancing. Edgar was so happy to watch her every move. She was like a flitting butterfly. Dancing to the vibrant cheerful folk tunes, she knew every move of the folk dances.

Linda watched Edgar watching Eva. She sipped her wine and thought of what a beautiful couple they would make. She would make sure they had every opportunity to be together so that it would happen. She winked at Mama. Mama winked back. They were already speaking that silent language that mothers have innately between them. They knew exactly what was happening between Edgar and Eva. With a wink, they made a pact to make sure to move things along.

The festivities went on until supper was served. The joy on the terrace was delightful. Sweat was pouring off Mama's brow. Papa was out of breath but, smiling ear to ear. Sandor and Rita did not want to stop. Eva sat out for the last couple of songs so that Prizi and Linda could hop on the floor. She sat and watched everyone, especially Edgar, with amazement. This was the most fun she had had in years.

Edgar played his heart out on the viola for her. He loved watching her dance. He wished he could jump out of the wheelchair and take her in his arms and dance all night with her. He thought she looked like an elegant ballerina while dancing. She gave it her all. Her energy and spirit were like a healing balm to his soul. He noticed that she had sat down to let Linda and Prizi dance. She was watching him. He put even more into his playing.

Linda asked Edgar to play a favorite song of his choice while the waiters were serving dinner. She wanted Eva to hear him play a solo. Mama already knew what a treat this was going to be. She could not wait for Eva to hear him.

He lifted the viola onto his left shoulder as if it were there from birth. The bow masterfully raised to strike the strings at the perfect time. He breathed in. On exhale he began. Of course, it was the best performance that he could muster because it was for Eva. He desperately wanted his playing to pierce her heart with every note. To show her the love he was beginning to have for her by giving his whole heart and soul while playing.

The family and guests were silent awaiting his first note. Everyone there had heard Edgar except for Eva. Everyone knew how gifted he was at the viola.

The bow lightly touched the strings. His eyes shut as if he was in a mystical dance with the universe bringing angelic sounds down from the heavens.

Linda looked at Eva and was thrilled. She knew that Eva was instantly captivated. Linda could not be happier. Mama saw the look on Eva's face. Mama knew for sure that this was most definitely going the right direction. Both Mothers sat back and enjoyed the story that was about to unfold.

Edgar played his favorite piece from Bach. Eva's interest in Edgar was growing with each note that he lovingly coaxed from the instrument. With every stroke of the bow her heart was taken in, like a captive to his enchantment.

"How could anyone play an instrument so well?" She thought.

It was as if his fingers were skipping like butterflies on the wind. The bow and strings were dancing together like sunshine glistening off a fast-flowing river. The gentle touch and kiss of the bow and strings, guided by his masterful strong hands, moved the notes along with delicate caresses and powerful passion.

She could picture playing her flute in a duet with him. Although she would be spellbound watching him the whole time. She could picture them sitting quietly by the river talking about anything and everything. Suddenly she could picture holding hands and stealing a kiss on the riverbank under the full moon. And in that fifteen minutes of him playing, as if he played with the gods of heaven guiding his hands, she had turned from a little girl to young lady falling in love. Desiring to be close to this handsome young man. She had never wanted to be close to a man before. All she had been interested in were her paintings, riding Lucy bareback, and fishing on the Tisza. Where did these thoughts come from?

The men kept drinking and were becoming more heated again with the talk of the latest politics, Opal, Linda and now even Rita had caught on to what the important work of the day was. They looked at each other with glee. They were already, in their minds, planning the wedding. They knew these two were meant for each other.

Soon dinner, dancing, and heated political conversations came to an end for the evening. New friendships had been made. New music had been heard. And love? Love was most definitely in the air. The three older women were determined to keep the fires stoked.

Chapter Six

First Kiss

Music: "Tea for Two" Art Tatum
"Love and Kisses" Ella Fitzgerald
"When the Saints Go Marching In" Louis Armstrong
History: March 23 The Slovak-Hungarian War begins.

The next day seemed like worlds away from what they experienced the night before. Back to work for everyone. Back to reality.

A couple weeks passed. Everyone in the village and wine region were busy enjoying the summer sun. Working hard in the fields. The Schwartz vineyard was buzzing with preparations for their summer season.

The butcher shop was filling orders and delivering all over the nearby villages. Lucy, Papa and the bright yellow delivery wagon were visible for miles. Everyone loved a visit from Papa. It was not just the fresh cuts of meat that they looked forward to. It was his genuine care for each neighbor and his sense of humor that they loved. He would perform little magic tricks for the small children at every stop. Pull a coin out from behind their ear. Make a rabbit out of a handkerchief. The children would run behind his cart as he pulled out onto the dirt roads. They would wave and yell, "Bye, Magic Man!" He would smile and wave goodbye, then nudge Lucy to giddy up. They would trot happily down the road knowing he had made the children happy once again.

It was late afternoon. Papa was done with deliveries. Mama saw, through the large front window of the shop, that Papa was on his way home. She was finishing chores at the counter. Papa and Lucy pulled the delivery wagon into the barnyard.

Eva's chores were done. "May I visit Edgar today?" Eva asked, "He might need something. Spending all day in the wheelchair must be hard."

Jokingly Mama said, "I'm sure his nurse can get things for him."

Eva rolled her eyes at her, "Mama, you know what I mean."

"I do?" Mama said with a grin, "Yes, you may go see Edgar. Don't be too late," Mama answered.

"Thank you," Eva said not wanting to go into a long conversation about visiting him. She did not know where this was going. She just knew she wanted to visit him.

Mama was more than happy to let her go. She *did* see where this was going.

Eva pulled off her apron as fast as she could. Flung her flute into her backpack. Dashed through the butcher shop door, as was her manner, and ran down the road towards the vineyard. She was hoping to be able to paint while listening to him play. Or play her flute with him.

Normally she would have ridden Lucy. Delivery days wore old Lucy out though. On delivery days Lucy needed to rest. Eva would run all the way over or borrow her other best friend and neighbor, Emily's, bicycle. Today she ran. Seemed faster. Love was in the air. She seemed to float all the way there.

War was also in the air and getting closer. Everyone felt the heaviness of it. No one knew what the future held. Eva was determined to make her future happy. And right now, at this moment, Edgar was making her very happy.

Eva arrived at the vineyard with a huge smile on her face. Edgar was waiting on the terrace. He was getting better at wheeling himself around in the cumbersome high back wheelchair. His broken leg is elevated on the foot pedal as much as possible. The cast made it stick straight out from the chair. It was from above his knee to his ankle. At first, he was dangerous and awkward with guiding the bulky wooden chair. He ran into all kinds of things around the house. Fortunately, nothing valuable had broken so far. He has gotten less dangerous with hitting things with his leg. Aunt Linda is fearful of the speed in which he flies around the house. She knows one day she will hear a crash of something from his maneuvers. She put up any glass valuables, just in case.

Edgar wished he could go to the butcher shop and pick Eva up on Rocky, instead of waiting for her to arrive. Linda had told him how much she loved riding Rocky. He would put that in his plans. He was a planner.

The doctor said Edgar's leg would be healed sometime in mid to late-August. He and Eva had the whole summer to slow down and get to know each other. After the cast was off, he would need to take a few weeks to do exercises to become stronger. He was a strong, robust, muscular young man from all the hard work on the farm. It would not take long to be back to normal. Eva assured him that she would help him through that.

Edgar wanted his parents Willis and Joan Holthaus in Düsseldorf to know how he was doing with his leg and with Eva. He was able to call them once a week when they were at his grandparents' home. They had a phone. He asked them about staying on at the vineyard until December to help with grape harvest and bottling. He told them he was in love and planned on asking Eva to marry him. He did not want to travel with the threat of war pressing down on them. They were sad that they would not be there for the wedding. They understood and of course gave their permission.

Joan was Aunt Linda's sister. She was Jewish. Her husband, Willis Holthaus, was German and Lutheran. They understood Edgar's plans. They did not think it would be safe for them to come to his wedding. They would prepare a homecoming for Edgar and Eva in December. Travel was restrictive and dangerous for everyone, especially Jews. Willis had to protect his wife from the chaos of Hitler's rage. They were both thrilled that Eva was Jewish.

Tonight though… on the wisteria vine draped terrace, with the brilliant sun drenching the skies, Edgar had something special planned, in case Eva did come over. He had something special planned every night for her. Eva hoped he would play the viola for her. She would leave her flute with him so she would not have to carry it every time. Edgar wanted to give Eva something incredibly wonderful. He had ordered it from a store in Tokaj. It arrived today. He could not hardly contain himself. He was so excited for her to open the package.

She was finally here. He could see her running up the long lane to the mansion. He saw her beautiful smile. She was in her bib overalls and black work boots. Her long black hair was flying in the wind. Edgar reached behind him for the blanket that was covering her surprise. He did not want her to see it right away.

Eva reached the wide granite steps of the terrace. She climbed the six steps to greet Edgar. His smile was unusually wide and mysterious. She reached out her hand to greet him. He always kissed her hand. She thought that was very romantic.

"How are you, sweetheart?" Edgar asked with confidence, thinking he should be calling her sweetheart by now.

"Sweetheart?" Eva asked with a blushed grin, liking the new pet name, surprised he was calling her that already. She allowed him to kiss her hand again. "What should I call you?" Eva asked playfully, not really expecting an answer.

"Husband?" Edgar said with an ornery grin.

"Oh, really?" Eva laughed. "You're moving a little too fast, aren't you?" She put her foot down, but not hard. She did like the sound of that. She did not want him to know that yet, though.

"I think we are going at just the right speed," He reassured her with another kiss on the hand, hoping he could get a kiss on the lips sometime.

"Did you have a good day?" Edgar asked, before he went to unveil the surprise.

"It was good. Busy. It was delivery day for Papa," She answered, curiously looking at Edgar, reaching for the blanket-covered lump on the table.

"I have a surprise for you," Edgar stated, too anxious to let it wait.

"You do?" answered Eva with a puzzled look on her face.

"I wanted to apologize for ruining your painting." Edgar explained before giving her the surprise.

"You didn't have to get me anything. I have forgiven you. I hope you forgave me for throwing paint on you and thumping you on the head with my paintbrush?" She cringed, never having brought it up to him before.

Edgar nodded and chuckled at her attempt for swift justice with her paint supplies. "Yes, I have. I deserved it." He pulled the blanket back slowly off of the gift and said, "I think you will like this."

"I'm sure I will, no matter what it is. Unless it's a snake or a spider," she laughed.

"No, I promise, I will never give you a snake or a spider," Edgar reassured her.

He pulled back the blanket. There was a large package wrapped in brown paper.

"Open it, please," he smiled and gestured.

Eva moved to the table and looked at the package then looked back at Edgar, "Thank you. Whatever it is, I'm sure I will love it."

She peeled back the paper gently so as not to ruin or tear what might be inside. Plus, she thought she could use the paper to paint on.

Once the paper was peeled back far enough that the gift was revealed, she squealed with delight. "No… it isn't… you didn't! This is the very first real easel that I have ever owned, except for the muddy stick ones that I made at the river."

"You're happy?" Edgar asked with much hope that she would love it.

"I don't think I've ever gotten such a wonderful gift. Yes, unexplainably happy. This is incredible," she gushed.

"I figured since I fell on your easel at the river and broke it and your painting, I'd get you a brand new, real one," Edgar explained.

"You really didn't have to," Eva answered with a gasp of unbelief.

"I know. But the joy on your face is all worth it," he answered with gratefulness. Edgar was overjoyed that she loved it.

Tears came welling up in Eva's eyes.

"I've never been given something so beautiful in all my life,"

"You deserve it, sweetheart," he said.

Eva bent down and kissed Edgar spontaneously on the cheek. They both looked at each other as she slowly pulled away. Their eyes were locked on each other for a second. They both wanted more than the kiss on the cheek. They both leaned in and kissed tenderly on the lips. She did not know what more to do other than that. She stepped away with the taste of his sweetness on her lips. Her innocence was adorable. He was ecstatic inside. He did not dare laugh or it would have given her the wrong idea, as if it was wrong to kiss or she did something wrong. It was all perfectly right. He loved it, and so did she. Their hearts were pounding fiercely. They did not know what to say. Silence was enough. Tears in both of their eyes were more than enough.

A few moments passed with their bodies gripped in momentary silent language of love that cannot be explained. Edgar picked up his viola and began to play. Eva was over the moon excited. After she caught her breath, she put her flute together and played along with him. They sat on the terrace until dusk, enjoying every note and every word they shared, holding hands in between songs.

Chapter Seven

Sitting on the Dock

Music: "I Thought About You" Mildred Bailey
"I Poured My Heart into a Song" Artie Shaw
History: March 31 - UK and France offer a guarantee of Polish independence. The Slovak-Hungarian War comes to an end.

It was easier to leave the easel at the vineyard than to carry it back and forth every day. "Sweetheart," as she was now known to Edgar, was so excited to tell Mama and Papa about the easel and everything. She talked nonstop the next few days about her visits with Edgar. Every customer in the shop got in on the conversations too. Suddenly, everyone in Tokaj knew the couple and were extremely happy they had found each other. Eva always shined. Now she was glowing.

It was not delivery day. Lucy was rested enough to ride. Eva hopped on her right after work. The backpack full of art supplies was always with her. She thought maybe she could paint while sitting with Edgar. It would be wonderous if he would play his viola while she painted.

"Maybe they could go to the vineyard's dock?" she thought, as she rode bareback on poor old Lucy. She discussed the matter with Lucy. Lucy seemed to agree. It was a huge dock with a lovely gazebo, right on the Tisza River. There were such beautiful scenic views to paint down there. She could push Edgar in his wheelchair down to the dock.

Lucy and Eva trotted down the long, tree-lined lane like clockwork. Edgar was sitting in his same faithful spot on the terrace waiting for them. Eva rode Lucy back to a clean stall at the barn before she went to the terrace. As she was putting Lucy in the stall that had been prepared for her by Linda, she saw Linda coming in from the fields on Rocky. Rocky was not decked out in his parade tack like Eva had seen him at the shop. Linda had been doing heavy work with him for the vineyard. Linda saw Eva putting Lucy up to feed and waved across the barnyard.

"Hey, my darling, will you be staying for supper?" Linda yelled loudly so she could hear her over the noisy barnyard.

"Yes, I'd love to. Thank you. How are you?" Eva asked, so happy to see Linda and Rocky.

Linda rode over to her. Eva and Rocky reconnected. She hugged his neck. He curled his wide strong neck, shiny mane, and head into her.

"You can ride him if you'd like," Linda said.

"Well, as tempting as that is, I have plans with Edgar," Eva explained. She turned to show Linda her backpack full of art supplies.

"So, you're more interested in Edgar than Rocky these days?" Linda asked with a smirk, knowing full well that that was the case. She had spied on them a little bit with Prizi when they had their first kiss. Eva kind of thought that might be the case, and she blushed when Linda asked her this question.

"Well… yes," Eva answered, then turned to Rocky and made sure his feelings were not hurt. "But you'll always be my favorite stallion." She patted him on the neck for reassurance. He nuzzled her sweetly.

"We heard Edgar gave you a new easel. I hope you like it?" Linda asked.

"It's the prettiest thing I've ever received," Eva answered with such gratefulness.

Linda was surprised and pleased that Eva thought so much of it. She did not realize it would have been the prettiest thing she had ever received.

"He wanted to make sure you have what you need for your painting. He knows how much you love it," Linda said, "Well, I've got to put Rocky up. I'll see you at supper."

"All right, see you soon," Eva answered, "Would it be okay if I took Edgar to the dock? I'm hoping he can play his viola down there while I paint."

"Of course, you may go anywhere you'd like to, my darling. This is your home too. You're family," Linda answered.

"Thank you so much," Eva was shocked at her generosity, so thankful to be accepted by this loving family.

Eva waved at Linda as she left the barn. Edgar was waiting patiently, viola on his lap. Ready to go. Grinning from ear to ear when he saw his gorgeous sweetheart walking toward him. Her bright smile captured his heart every time he saw her.

"Hello, Sweetheart," he said again. It sounded better every time he said it. He loved how it sounded. He loved seeing her smile when he said it.

"Hello, Sweetheart," Eva said back to him for the first time. Oh, how he loved hearing that. Mostly because he had been thinking of their future and he wanted to make sure she was okay to talk about a future with him.

"Did you have a good day?" Eva asked.

"I did. I hope you did too?" Edgar answered.

"I did. Good day at the shop. Not too busy. Just steady," Eva answered. Then hesitated, "I think everyone in town knows we are a couple now."

"Oh, so we ARE a couple now, are we?" Edgar slyly asked.

"I-I think we are," stammered Eva, just to check herself on what all of that meant.

"I think we are too. I couldn't be happier that we are. I feel so fortunate that I found you. I hope I make you happy too?" Edgar asked.

"I've never been happier," Eva answered with a deep soothing sigh.

"I'm glad you had a good day at work. I can't wait to get back to work," Edgar mentioned, "I miss getting out in the vineyard and helping on the farm."

"I'm sure you do," Eva said in a very understanding tone, "I have an idea for something different we could do today."

"Sounds great. What do you have in mind?" Edgar asked with anticipation.

"Would you like to go to the dock? I brought my paints. I can set up the easel and paint, and we can talk. You can play the viola if you'd like," Eva asked, hoping he would.

"That sounds wonderful. Do you trust me to be around you when you are painting down by the river?" he asked with a wink.

"As long as you're not falling out of a rotten tree, I think we'll be alright," Eva laughed.

Oh, how he loved to make her laugh. She sounded so sweet when she laughed.

Edgar had the easel set up on the terrace. He put it and the viola case on his lap. Eva pushed him slowly over the bumpy dirt path down to the wide lovely dock. She almost spilled him, and all he was carrying, twice. All they could do was laugh at each other. They were determined to get to the dock and enjoy the beautiful view of the waters of the Tisza.

They set up Eva's new art area under the large elaborate gazebo. The gazebo was big enough to throw a party for about thirty to forty people. The

Schwartzes loved throwing parties on the gazebo. They loved throwing parties anywhere on their vineyard. Edgar began to play the viola while Eva painted.

Linda and Prizi stood on the balcony of their bedroom watching the young couple for a few minutes. They enjoyed listening to the mesmerizing sound of Edgar's viola playing. The notes floated on the air, up the hill, all the way up to the mansion. Their balcony doors were open so they could listen to his music. They went inside so as not to be spying on the lovely couple.

After about half an hour of playing, Edgar took a break and watched Eva paint. He felt like he could do that all day. It brought him back to the very first moment that he saw her. He could not believe how lucky he was to have her in his life. He knew he had to talk with her and see what she thought about the future. He had some plans that were already in place with the Düsseldorf Symphony and possibly the New York Symphony that he wanted her to know about.

"Eva?" he spoke almost reluctantly, hoping this conversation did not turn her away from him.

"Yes," she turned from her painting and the river to answer him.

"Could we talk about the future, our future?"

"I've always thought we can never know what the future holds," she answered with a smirk, knowing full well where this was going.

She looked at him and saw that he had a serious look on his face. She sat down on the bench next to him and put her paints to the side. She felt like this was going to be a serious conversation.

He appreciated that she understood that it was serious without him having to tell her. He wanted them to be on the same page with their hearts and minds.

"Do you think that we could be in a committed relationship?"

Without hesitating, Eva said, "Yes, but how serious are you thinking? You're always way ahead of me."

"I'd like to think marriage," Edgar said hoping she would at least not faint when he said it.

"Well, this is extremely fast. I'd have to think more about it," Eva said with some surprise at how fast Edgar was approaching this subject, "Why are you in a hurry?"

"I wouldn't be in such a hurry, except for the possible approaching war and the offer that I've had from the Düsseldorf Symphony Orchestra and the New York Symphony Orchestra. If it were just me, I know where and what I would be doing without question. I want you to be with me, if you want to be," Edgar began his explanation.

"What do you mean? War? Symphonies?" Eva asked, only having pictured them staying in Tokaj the rest of their lives near family. She would have loved to live in Paris, as was her childhood dream, but once she knew this relationship was going the direction it was going with Edgar, she set that dream aside for a while. She would be just as happy with a little cottage on the river, painting the rest of her days with him by her side.

"You know I'm from Düsseldorf. What I haven't told you is that I've been studying viola with a mentor since I was four years old. They called me a prodigy. I just like playing. I never really knew how good I was until after a few years of playing I was considered one of the best violists in Germany. I was invited to play with the symphony on a full-time basis when I go home this year after grape harvest. The other opportunity is with the New York Symphony. They heard me play and have offered me a full-time position anytime I want to take it. We are Jewish, Eva. Even though you are a Hungarian Jew, I don't think that will save you. Our Jewish roots run too deep, and I have a bad feeling about what may be coming at us," Edgar explained.

Eva paused, dropped her head to think a moment, then said, "I've already lost my parents. My grandparents are all I have. I thought I would take care of them in their old age. I don't know what to tell you."

"I understand. It's a lot to think about. The war is approaching. My parents are afraid of what Hitler may be planning. They call and send letters with information that keep me up to date with what is happening in Germany. I'm not asking you for an answer right now. I'm just starting a conversation so we can be prepared for whatever happens."

"Right. That's understandable. I believe I want to be with you. I do not want to leave here. What if we stay here through grape harvest and see how things go?" Eva mustered her reply from her frightened heart.

"That sounds like a great idea. With Hungary still being in alliance with Germany we may be spared for a while. We'll take it day by day and see how things develop. I'll call my parents and see if that sounds safe to them," Edgar replied with an open heart and mind.

"Tell me more about playing with the symphonies. Is that your dream, to play for Düsseldorf and maybe New York?" Eva asked.

"Düsseldorf would be my dream. I could be close to family and play viola the rest of my life. I would love that. To have you by my side would make it perfect. New York was never even a thought on my list of things to do. However, New York's offer may be the right move if it gets necessary to leave

Europe. Would you be willing to take that risk with me? It is a very prestigious offer. It might be our only means of escape if things go really bad." Edgar said, trying to be realistic but not scare Eva.

"I'd have to think about it. These are tough decisions. I can't make them right now. I do appreciate your thoughtfulness in thinking about our future though. I would love to have that with you," Eva answered with firm conviction.

Edgar breathed a sigh of relief, "That makes my heart feel at peace, Eva. I'm glad we talked about these things."

"Me too," She said, "Hey, it's almost time for supper. I'll leave my easel here. Linda invited me for supper. It will take me a while to push you up the hill."

"I'll help push the wheels."

"You'd better. I don't know if I can get you up there," Eva laughed with a "heave-ho" in her voice.

Chapter Eight

Prizi's Announcement

Music: "What's New?" Bing Crosby

"Take My Hand, Precious Lord" Mahalia Jackson

History: April 3 - Hitler orders the German military to begin planning for Fall Weiss. This is the codename for the attack on Poland. It was secretly planned to be launched on August 25, 1939.

"Here they come," yelled Sandor from the terrace.

The cousins ran down to help Eva push the wheelchair. They grabbed the viola to relieve Edgar from carrying it. He helped turn the wheels to take the weight off of pushing him.

"Thank you so much," Eva said to the boys, as she let go of the wheelchair and let Daniel push Edgar the rest of the way.

"No problem," answered Samuel. "We know he can be a burden."

The other boys laughed in agreement.

Edgar took a swipe at Sam with his big muscular arms. He laughed and jumped out of the way.

"You know I can kick your ass, Sam," Edgar said, chuckling at how fast he had moved.

"That's true," Daniel said, "but only if you can catch him."

"Yeah, you'd better watch out, Sam. He's kicked your ass many times," warned Akos, the youngest sibling.

Peter and Padraig, the twins, smacked Edgar on the head as they ran by. Padraig was carrying the viola. They ran ahead of the others to get to the terrace before Edgar took another swing at them.

"What am I listening to?" Linda asked, standing on the edge of the terrace stairs, knowing full well how mischievous the boys are and how wildly they talk to one another. "Rita and I have just made a new batch of lye soap, and I have a good mind to wash your mouths out with it."

The boys would not put it past her. They also knew she was kidding… this time. They straightened up their act and fell into place. Apologizing to their strong Momma, they hoisted Edgar up the stairs, then marched like little obedient soldiers by her so she would not make good on that promise. The taste of lye soap sticks with you. They knew they did not want to taste that again. She stood with arms crossed, shaking her head at each of them as they passed. And, yes, her fierce Momma eyes were on each one.

Eva got a little chuckle at how well Linda commanded this unruly crew. She was definitely the "little general" of the family. Each son marched passed her as if they were her troop of soldiers. They knew who was in charge. She gave each one of them a good solid pat on the butt as they passed by. They knew it could be harder if she really meant it.

"Everyone, grab a chair," Linda instructed. "Rita has made a delicious meal for us. Your father has some news for you."

Sandor and Rita lived in a tiny chalet on the vineyard. They usually ate meals with them.

Everyone was seated and enjoying the meal. The boys were thanking Rita for her delicious fisherman's soup full of fish from the local river and her scrumptious dessert, plum pudding.

Prizi finished his meal and started to prepare the family for the news. Linda, Rita, and Sandor were a bit anxious about the news. They already knew what was coming. It would mean a lot harder work for all of them.

"Boys, this summer we're going to need you to focus and work harder than ever," Prizi began.

A huge sigh from the boys went out and muttering began. They were worried about what that meant. They felt like they were already working as hard as they could. They looked at each other and wondered where this was going.

Edgar sunk in his chair a bit. He felt like he was not helping at all, that he was a burden to them.

Prizi saw the look on their faces. He wanted to reassure them that he and Linda would be working right along with them as hard as they could too.

"I've hired two more experienced workers to help us," Prizi said.

The boys wanted to ask why they needed two more workers. They knew to wait. He would explain everything.

"Our neighbors, the Kovacs, just lost their Father in a farming accident. They're going to need us to pitch in and help with their vineyard." Prizi began his explanation.

The boys wanted to complain. They knew that they better not because it was only right for them to help their neighbors in their time of need. Their neighbors would do the same for them.

"Is there anything I can do to help?" Edgar asked earnestly so he would not feel like a burden to them.

"We will find some things for you to help with. We're going to need all hands-on deck," Prizi confirmed, "You can help with the bookkeeping for both vineyards. You're good with numbers."

"Yes, sir," Edgar answered in relief.

Eva knew these neighbors too. They were customers at the shop. She decided that she would help with the vineyard as much as she could too. She would ask Mama and Papa about it when she got home. Her life was going in the direction of being with Edgar, so she needed to plan accordingly.

"Does anyone have any questions?" Prizi asked.

There was a pause after he asked because everyone knew the plan. They knew it had to be done.

After a short silence and letting this news settle in, Sandor had a question, "Have you thought anymore about building shelters in the wine cellars in case the war reaches us?"

"I have thought about it. I'm afraid we have more pressing matters than that, now that our neighbors need our help. We could possibly set up a very quick primitive kind of shelter in a couple of the cellars. That will have to be put on hold for now though," Prizi answered.

Sandor answered silently with a sad understanding nod. He looked at Rita while she was clearing dishes. They had both been through WWI. They knew the atrocities of war. They knew they needed to prepare for the worst even if it never came. They were feeling in their bones the heaviness in the air. The preparations would give them some peace. Sandor decided he would work on a shelter as he had extra time in their private underground wine cellar. Almost every family in Tokaj had their own private underground wine cellar. It did not look like there would be much extra time with this new workload upon them. He could put a few minutes a day on the project. It would be something to give them both a little peace of mind. Rita looked back at Sandor and nodded as if she knew everything he was thinking. She probably did. They had been together for forty years.

"No worries, Boss. We'll do our best with what we've been given," Sandor answered with respect.

Rita quietly walked to the kitchen with the help of Linda and Eva. The three of them cleared the dishes and let Prizi fill the men in with the details of their duties.

Edgar watched as Eva walked away. He wanted this to be a time when he could have told his family of their tentative plans. He would save it for another day. They were only tentative anyway. Nothing was set in stone. "Stone," he thought. "That's it." He needed to get her a stone as soon as possible. Things were moving along faster than he expected. He could not afford a diamond. He had a great idea. He would have to ask Sandor for help. Even though Sandor was terribly busy, he knew he would want to help him with this.

The evening came to an end. There was just enough light to get Lucy back to the shop and brush her out before it became too dark. Eva said her goodbyes to everyone. Instead of being embarrassed and kissing Edgar in front of everyone, she held out her hand and he kissed it. All the boys whooped and whistled at them. She turned red. Edgar just winked at her. As if to say, "Don't pay any attention to their shenanigans."

Linda gave them all a funny look. That did not stop them. This was bigger than the little general could control. They never gave up a chance to tease each other. They were all susceptible to a good ribbing. It was just Edgar's turn today. They kept it up until Edgar and Eva turned completely red.

Eva looked at Linda as if to say, "Will this last forever?"

Linda smiled back at her and shrugged her shoulders, giving her the silent signal saying, "Probably."

Sandor had gotten Lucy ready for Eva and walked her up to the terrace. Eva hopped on and rode away. Edgar watched every moment until she was out of sight. Linda did not say a word. She did not have to. Love was in the air. It was just too bad that war was too.

Supper was wonderful as usual. The cousins were rowdy as ever. Eva was more comfortable with them and fit right in with her ornery sense of humor. Linda and Prizi were so happy with how well she fit in with the family.

Edgar and Eva did not mention anything to the family about their talk of future plans. They did not want to cause the family any concern.

Eva got home a little after dark. Mama and Papa were not worried. They knew she was safe and growing into her new family situation.

Eva brushed Lucy out and put in her stall. Eva took a long soaking bath and thought about all that her and Edgar had talked about. She realized life was going to change for all of them in one way or another very soon.

Chapter Nine

The Rock

Music: "Our Love" Tommy Dorsey
"A-Tisket A-Tasket" Ella Fitzgerald

History: April 4 - Hungary and Slovakia sign the Budapest Treaty. This handed over a strip of eastern Slovak territory to Hungary.

The sun was rising over the mountains of Tokaj. Streams of prism colors came sparkling through the six-foot bevel tiled windows in the foyer of the mansion. The window looked out over the vineyards. Staring out the window, Edgar gazed at row after row of manicured glistening grapevines. They stretched out in perfect parallel lines below the mansion. The mansion sits on a hill and looks down on the patchwork quilt of fields. Morning dew was drizzled on the long straight rows, like crystals sparkling in the dawn sun. Outside the mansion's gate, the vines run in straight rows all the way up to the mountains.

Dahlia, Edgar's strong, stout nurse, should be here soon. He wanted to get an early start on his project. The ground would be a little softer to dig into in the morning. The night before he had asked Dahlia if she could show up a little earlier than usual. Of course, she would. She loved Edgar like a son. He did not tell her what they were going to do. She was well known in town and could have spread the word to everyone out of excitement. He wanted to keep it a secret.

"Good morning," Edgar greeted Dahlia, opening the massive carved oak door for her. He sat in his wheelchair with a shovel on his lap. This was looking quite curious to Dahlia.

"Well, good morning, Edgar. How did you get dressed?" Dahlia asked.

"I'm getting better at it. Linda helped me with the parts I couldn't manage myself," Edgar answered with triumph in his voice.

"You sound excited today. What is this all about?" Dahlia asked, with fascination in her voice. She was happy to see him making progress. She was still curious as to why he had a shovel on his lap.

"I can't tell you right now. I just need your help to go to our fields and find a very pretty piece of volcanic rock," Edgar answered, with no intention of giving her a full explanation.

Dahlia laughed, "There's volcanic rock all over these hills and valleys. That's what these mountains are made of. What are you up to?" Dahlia could have never imagined why he needed it. It made her chuckle that it was so important to him to find a pretty rock. She just shook her head and pushed him out to the closest field.

"I didn't know part of my duties was hunting rocks or I would've packed a shovel in my medical bag," Dahlia said with a chuckle.

"You'll have to add that to your resumé. It could get you some interesting jobs in the future," Edgar laughed, assisting her by pushing the wheels while she helped him out to the vineyard.

Out they went to a very pretty spot in the middle of the closest field. Edgar did not want to go too far. It was enough to ask Dahlia to do this for him. He did not want her to work too hard pushing him.

"I think I can dig a little dirt away and shovel some to see if I can find a small stone," Edgar said, scraping at the soil. Dahlia offered to help him dig. He thanked her but thought he wanted to do it himself.

After a few small shovelfuls and examining many small stones, he found the one he wanted. He took some extra ones just in case that one did not work out. Dahlia pushed him back to the house still wondering what this was all about.

He hoped Sandor could help him. With the extra work that has been added to the workers, he hated to ask him. He also knew that Sandor would want to be the one to help him with this special project. Sandor knew how to weld and do metal work finer than anyone in the area. The stone would need to come from Tokaj soil. That would mean more to Eva than a diamond at this time. Besides, Edgar could not afford a diamond yet. Volcanic rock is the most prevalent stone in the area. That would be symbolic and sentimental to her. He could get a diamond when they got to New York. He would be making a better income. He decided this engagement ring would be made of a small piece of volcanic rock that the area was famous for. She would always have a piece of Tokaj with her no matter where they went.

At dinner that night Edgar gave the tiny stones and his gold cufflinks that the Düsseldorf Symphony had awarded him to Sandor. He explained what he was wanting to do with them. He asked Linda if she could figure out what size ring Eva wore. She happily agreed and would secretly find out with Opal's help.

Everyone in the two families were in on Edgar's plan, except Eva. Once Linda took it on as her mission to help him, she made sure her sister- and brother-in-law were in on it too.

Sandor and Rita were very willing to help make the rings. Rita had a small fresh-water pearl that Sandor had found on a fishing trip on the Tisza river. She offered it to Edgar to put in the setting of the ring. Edgar gladly and humbly accepted. That would also remind Eva of the area and where they first met.

It would not take too long to make the rings. Sandor was a great craftsman. He would make the molds and set the stones and pearl as soon as Linda found out what size she wore.

One week into August Sandor had the rings ready. They were perfect. He used two pieces of volcanic rock that he had polished to perfection and surrounded the pearl with them. It was beautiful. Linda, Opal, and Rita cried when they saw it. That is when Sandor knew he had gotten it right. Edgar could not believe he had made one for him too. It was a thin piece of gold that he had left over from the cufflinks with a tiny polished volcanic stone set in it. Edgar teared up and thanked him endlessly.

Linda and Prizi decided to have a dinner for the occasion of the proposal. Dahlia was invited to the dinner. She had been helping Edgar practice getting stronger. Helping him bend to get down on one knee. He had finally let her in on his secret. He swore her to secrecy. It was desperately hard for her to keep the secret. She did concede to his wishes, for the most part.

Dinner was planned for the entire family the next evening. Everyone knew what was going to happen, except Eva. Everyone came from work as usual so Eva would not expect anything. The boys were just as rowdy as ever. No one had changed out of their work clothes. They did not want anything to tip her off as to what was about to happen.

Edgar would like to get married at the end of August. The war rumors were ramping up. He knew their safest bet would be to get to New York. That would not give them much time to prepare a wedding. He was hoping that did not matter to Eva.

Dinner was almost done. Everyone was sitting, patiently waiting for the moment. Eva wondered why Dahlia, Mama and Papa were here. Linda loved having guests. So, she figured it was an almost normal night at the Schwartzes. They tended to have those almost-normal nights a lot.

Suddenly, it got noticeably quiet. Eva looked up from her dessert. She did not know what was going on. Everyone was staring at her. Feeling self-conscious, she put her fork down and swallowed the piece of apricot kolache whole, almost choking due to not really chewing it first. She turned to Edgar. He had pushed himself away from the table. He was rising up out of his wheelchair by pushing himself upwards on the arms of the chair. Two of his cousins that were closest to him, Samuel and Daniel, stood on either side of him in case he fell. All the practice Dahlia did with him was paying off. Dahlia was so happy she was about to burst. Eva looked at this situation with awkward curiosity. She had no idea what to make of it. Edgar lowered himself slowly and carefully to the ground on his good knee. The leg with the cast was out in front of him. He reached into his shirt pocket and pulled out the old ring box that Sandor and Rita had put the ring in. It was borrowed from their wedding rings. He opened it and asked the question.

"Would you, my love, my sweetheart Eva, do me the honor of marrying me?" Edgar asked.

Everyone at the table was so still. They were frozen in place. Collectively inhaled. No one could breathe until she said yes.

Eva was in shock. She did not see it coming this soon. She stuttered at first. She could not get the word out.

"Y-y-yes, of course I will," she finally answered.

A collective exhale went around the table. The boys started whooping and yelling. The ladies were crying and hugging. The men's eyes were misting up, and they were shaking hands. Cigars were passed. Drinks were poured. Edgar and Eva… they were staring hopelessly in love into each other's eyes, holding on to every second of this glorious moment.

Edgar let out a huge sigh. He was so happy. Eva reached down to hug him. She gave him a nice long kiss. Samuel and Daniel helped him back to the wheelchair. They gave him hearty pats on the back. Then they both let out loud screams of happiness. Everyone clapped and cheered. They would all be family. Tears rolled for everyone. The boys grabbed their musical instruments and played to celebrate. Everyone began to dance. This was the happiest all of them had been in an awfully long time.

"It's beautiful," Eva said in thankfulness of the ring that fit her perfectly. "How did you know what size I wear? I don't even know what size I wear. What are these stones?"

"Linda and Mama figured out what size you wore," Edgar explained, "The stones are volcanic rock from the hills of Tokaj. Rita added a fresh-water pearl that Sandor found while fishing on the Tisza."

Tears came to Eva's eyes. Edgar could not be happier.

"I don't know what to say. It's beautiful. We're engaged! I couldn't be happier," Eva exclaimed with another hug and kiss.

"I'm so happy, Eva," Edgar told his new fiancée. "I couldn't afford a diamond right now. I thought you would like a piece of Tokaj with you wherever we go. Sandor made it."

"I love it. It's absolutely perfect, Sweetheart. The thoughtfulness involved in it is priceless. Thank you, Sandor and Rita," Eva exclaimed, hugging him as tight as she ever had.

"You are perfect, Sweetheart." Edgar pulled her closer to him. He did not know if life could get any better than this moment.

Chapter Ten

Big City

Music: "The Lion Sleeps Tonight" Solomon Linda & the Evening Birds "Lester Leaps In" Count Basie

History: April 14 - President Roosevelt sends letter to German Chancellor Hitler and Italian Prime Minister Mussolini seeking peace.

Josephine Baker: September 1939, France declared war on Germany in response to the invasion of Poland, Baker was recruited by the Deuxième Bureau, French military intelligence, as an "honorable correspondent." Baker collected the information that she could about German military locations from officials she met at parties. She specialized in gatherings at embassies and ministries, charming everyone as she had always done, while gathering information. Her café-society notoriety enabled her to rub shoulders with those in the know, from high-ranking Japanese officials to Italian bureaucrats, and to report what she heard. She attended parties and gathered information at the Italian embassy without raising suspicion. Ernest Hemingway called her "the most sensational woman anyone ever saw."

It was time for Edgar to have his leg x-rayed. Eva and Linda were right by his side. They traveled by train to the closest city that Dr. Nagy advised them to go to.

Linda and Edgar were excited for Eva to see a big city. If all went well, they could have lunch in a beautiful marketplace or outdoor café. Maybe take in a little shopping after Edgar's x-ray.

The idea of a train ride was exciting but hard for Eva. She rarely got out of Tokaj. She had a fear of trains since the train wreck that took her parent's lives. She knew she needed to fight through those feelings. She did not bring it up to Linda or Edgar. Opal reminded Linda about it so she could keep an eye out for her during their travels.

The train sped and sometimes chugged past some stunning Hungarian landscape. Eva was enthralled by all of it.

"I can't believe the beautiful sites. The farmers working in their fields, mountains and rivers" Eva stated as she looked out the train window. Hungary is gorgeous."

"I love the country. Wait until you see the city. You're going to fall in love with it too, Eva," Linda said with fun anticipation in her voice.

"I love both country and city. We'll find some wonderful things to do in the city." Edgar said with enthusiasm.

After their long ride, the train came to a stop at the massive elaborate station. Eva was awestruck with the beauty and immense size of the structure.

The ladies took turns pushing Edgar to the hospital. It was only a few blocks away from the train station. Once inside, their wait was not too long. Dr. Nagy had called ahead to help their process go as smooth as possible. He had gone to school with Dr. Simon. He was like a brother to him. Dr. Simon had gone on to specialize in orthopedics. The x-ray was taken. Dr. Simon would come back to get them as soon as he read it.

The three of them went back to the waiting room. There was a conversation going on in the waiting room that changed the direction of their whole day and possibly their whole lives. They could not help but listen to the gruff older man seated across from them. He was spouting off about his feelings about Jews in Hungary to the younger man, who was Jewish, seated next to him. By the time, they sat down it had already gotten heated. The nurse at the desk was disgusted by him. She gave Linda, Eva, and Edgar a look like, "What can I do?"

"I fought in WWI," yelled the older man. "We don't need any more fights. All of you Jews need to do is get out of Hungary. You are nothing but trouble. You take all our jobs. The Germans should erase you from the earth."

The nurse came out from behind her desk and tried to politely shut the man up. She directed him into one of the rooms down the hall. Slowly, walking with his cane, he shouted at the young man until he got into the room. The nurse shut the door.

The frazzled nurse came back into the waiting room. She saw the shocked look on everyone's faces. The young man that was being yelled out left the office. Eva was especially frightened. She had never heard anyone talk so hatefully, especially against Jewish people, her people. Her skin was crawling. She did not want to cry. She did not want to show fear. She sat straight up and tried to show strength in a horrible situation.

Edgar and Linda had touted the glamourous lifestyle of being in the city. She had always wanted to go to Paris. Was this what life was like outside of Tokaj? She was in disbelief. She felt like she had been kicked in the stomach.

"So sorry for that terrible disruption," the nurse said apologetically to everyone in the waiting room.

She was completely embarrassed by his words. She went back to sit at her desk. She had no explanation. She did not seem to want to talk about it. No one did.

"Are you okay?" Edgar whispered to Eva.

"I will be," Eva answered. "Can we go home right after this?"

"Of course," Linda answered, putting her arm around her and hugging her into her to comfort her like a daughter. "I'm so sorry you had to hear that hatred."

A few moments passed. They sat quietly thinking about it. Eva finally spoke.

"This city can't be *full* of hate. You have both said how much you love cities. We can't let one person stop us from what we want to do in life. Let's have lunch and enjoy our day here. If we allow others to control us, we will live in fear our whole lives," Eva said with deep conviction.

Linda and Edgar looked at each other in surprise and were convicted with her. They both loved her now more than ever.

"All right, we will do exactly that," Edgar agreed.

Linda nodded in agreement with both. "You're right, Eva. You're exactly right."

Next thing they knew, they heard the old man coming down the hall. The doctor was right behind him. The doctor had been with the man and heard his rhetoric. Dr. Simon was ushering him out and told him to never come back to his office.

Everyone in the waiting room, including the nurse, applauded in agreement when the doctor closed the door on the man. He turned around to continue his work, shaking his head in unbelief. His mother was Jewish. Edgar noticed the doctor was tearing up as he came up to him. Dr. Simon caught himself and regained his composure to address his patients.

"Well, that was unnecessary," spoke Doctor Simon, regretting that that had happened in his office. "Edgar, can you come back to the examination room?"

"Yes, sir," Edgar answered with much respect. "May my family come with me?"

"Yes, of course," answered the Doctor, still a bit out of sorts.

When they got to the examination room, the news was great. Edgar was healing perfectly. The new cast could come off by the third week in August.

"Do you have any plans for the rest of the summer?" asked the doctor.

Eva and Edgar both smiled as if sunshine was bursting from their pores.

"Yes, sir, we're getting married. We'll be having a wedding as soon as I can walk down the aisle," Edgar explained.

"I can see the joy in your faces," Dr. Simon answered, now smiling with them, "Just keep doing what you're doing. That cast will be off in no time. Have Dr. Nagy take it off for you. Tell him hi for me. Tell him he owes me a backgammon game," the Doctor instructed. "You'll be down that aisle in no time."

"Great, thank you, I will," Edgar answered, shaking his hand in thankfulness for the assessment and gratitude for the doctor taking a stand with that rude man.

They said their goodbyes to brave Dr. Simon and his nurse. Then, went to enjoy the rest of their day. They had lunch at a picturesque outdoor café. Shopping was next on their agenda. Wedding dresses were at the top of the list to shop for. Although they could not afford a new wedding dress, they were thrilled to shop for them. To see what the latest styles were.

The party of three enjoyed the next few hours in the beautiful outdoor markets and restaurants. Eva felt like she had been transported to Paris. She had no idea there were such lovely cities in Hungary.

The train ride back to Tokaj was at dusk. Eva was enjoying the Hungarian countryside as the sun went down. She would never forget the hate that that man in the doctor's office was spewing. She would never allow any hate to keep her from doing what she needed to do in life. As she watched the breathtaking scenery go by the train window, she made that vow to herself.

Chapter Eleven

Under the Chuppah

Music: "Faithful Forever" Glenn Miller

"Moon Love" Glenn Miller

History: September 1, 1939, first day of WWII. Germany invades Poland.

The Rabbi was called.

The wedding was set for Thursday, August 31.

They did not have much time to put a wedding together. From what the family in Tokaj and in Düsseldorf were hearing, speed was of the necessity for everyone's safety.

With two farms to work and harvest, this wedding was important, but it needed to be simple, quick, and gorgeous, no problem for the matriarchs of the family and the community. With Opal, Linda and Rita leading all the hard-working ladies of the community, they would make it an event for everyone to remember. Everyone in the area needed a festive get-together. By hook or by crook they were going to make it happen for the couple and the entire farming community.

Edgar's family from Düsseldorf was not going to be able to make it. They decided the hostile political climate would be too dangerous for them to travel. They would celebrate with the newlyweds when they moved to Düsseldorf. It would be easier for Eva to travel once she had a German last name.

Edgar was extremely sad that his father, mother and sister would not be able to be at the wedding. He would miss his father walking him down to the chuppah. Uncle Prizi and Lawrence would walk him to the chuppah. Opal and Linda would walk Eva to the chuppah. The Orthodox Jewish traditions would be done as best they could without Edgar's family present. The cousins would play the music. The wedding would be small and simple, held at the mansion.

The decorations would be from the natural foliage found around the vineyard. Everyone in the family and staff gathered grapevine clippings, roses from the flourishing rose gardens, evergreen from the nearby forest. Ladies from the Temple volunteered to make ropes and bundles out of the foliage for centerpieces and other decorations. They tied them with ribbons donated from ladies and girls in town. They also used satin strips of the leftover train from Eva's wedding dress.

The ropes of evergreen, vines, and roses not only brightened up the foyer and terrace, their aroma was heavenly throughout the wedding and reception areas. They were draped down the tall curving intricately carved, banister that swept through the two-story foyer. Eva would make her entrance from the top of the massive, stunning staircase. The matching bundles of flowers and centerpieces went from the foyer into the terrace where the reception was held. The scent of evergreens and roses sweetly filled the air.

The Dress… Eva could not afford the dresses they saw when they went shopping in the city. They did get some ideas for making one. Or, refurbishing one. Mama knew she would not want anything except for her Mom's wedding dress. Eva was much taller than her mother. The dress had damage on the arms and the train. Mama was not that good of a seamstress to fix it. Linda was. They cut the sleeves down to three-quarter length. They saved what they could from the remnants and made ribbons for Eva and her two best friends, bridesmaids, Helena and Emily's hair. Helena was able to wear her nice pink dress for the bridesmaid's dress. The one Eva had borrowed the first time she visited the mansion. Helena and Eva were able to get the mud out of it. Emily had a lovely red dress that matched the roses in the bouquet and other foliage used for decoration. The bride and both bridesmaids looked glorious. Helena's long light brown hair was laced with ribbons, baby's breath and pink rose pedals to match her dress. Her smile was brightened with pink lipstick and light rouge on her beautiful cheeks. Emily's bright blonde hair was pulled up in a soft bun with ribbons, baby's breath and red rose pedals perfectly placed to match her dress. Her enormous genuine smile was enhanced by red lipstick and a touch of rouge that Linda placed perfectly on her gorgeous complexion. They were both stunning. Eva was so thankful that both her best friends were sharing her special day with her. She could not have done it without them. Linda's wedding dress became the extra pieces that they needed to make Eva's dress complete. Both Linda's and Eva's mother's dresses were made of satin. Linda and Mama miraculously made it work. It looked like it came out of a designer's showroom in Paris. The wedding dress fit Eva perfectly. It made her feel like her parents were there.

The men wore their dashing traditional Hungarian folk wear that they wore when they played their instruments for festivals. It was going to be a festive and colorful wedding.

The guests were customers of the vineyard, butcher shop, and the congregation from the Temple. So… basically the entire town of Tokaj.

A feast of meats and a vast assortment of wines were being prepared to be served. Ladies from town, neighbors, friends, made the wedding cake and brought other favorite desserts.

Gifts of cash came from everyone. They knew part of the plans for the new couple. They knew they were moving to Düsseldorf. They did not know that they planned on escaping Europe to New York City.

Eva, Mama, Linda, Emily, and Helena were upstairs in Linda's bedroom getting ready for the walk down the grand staircase to the chuppah. The last of the makeup was put on. Mama could hardly hold back her tears looking at Eva in her mother's dress. Linda was so happy to have a new daughter in the family. Emily, Helena, and Eva were jumping up and down hugging each other with happiness. Mama made them stop or they would ruin their dresses and make-up.

Eva went to stand by the tall window to be quiet for a few moments before the procession began. In that quiet moment, by herself, she looked out at the people coming into the mansion. The bedroom window overlooked the driveway. Eva saw the cars and horse drawn carriages that were lined up. They were full of people coming to see her and Edgar get married. She wanted her mother and Father here so badly. She did feel like they were here in her heart. Mama had sewn in part of Eva's father's prayer shawl into the inner lining of the dress. Eva felt it on her waist and touched it often to acknowledge his presence.

The guests looked astounding. The men with their tall hats and best suits. The women wearing their best dresses. Some had darling hats. Some were wearing fur-trimmed jackets. Some were dressed in the best cotton dresses they had made themselves. The children were hopping, skipping, and giggling all the way up to the beautifully adorned entrance. Eva knew every person that was entering the home. It was such a magical gathering already. She could not wait for the wedding and reception to begin.

One last song was playing that the bridesmaids would walk down to, before the music changed to the wedding march. The boys were doing such a fine job of playing the music so sweetly.

Helena and Emily gave Eva big hugs and kisses. It was time for them to go. They began to walk towards the top of the stairs for their entrance down to the main floor. They looked at each other with words that did not need to be spoken. They were both overtaken by the exquisite sight of all the guests seated below. Everyone was dressed extremely sharp. The foyer was breathtaking. The candles were lit. The foliage draped over the curved banister. It was all so gracefully grand.

The chuppah was filled with men with smiles that could not be described accurately. They were so brilliant that their smiles outshined the candles surrounding them. Helena and Emily walked down beautifully, one after the other. Two beautiful Hungarian girls, schoolmates that had known Eva since childhood. Now, the three of them, all grown up. They reached their destination and waited for their best friend to enter the room.

The music changed to the wedding march. The boys had some extra help from a quartet from Tokaj with this piece. Mama and Linda were on either side of Eva holding her by each arm. They guided her to the top of the stairs. Mama and Linda gave Eva a squeeze on each elbow when they got to the top of the stairs. They were all taken back by the brilliance of the scene, just as Helena and Emily had been. As if they had practiced it, they both gave Eva a gentle kiss through the delicate veil to let her know how much they loved her before she took off on this new journey in her and Edgar's lives.

Edgar stood under the chuppah waiting for Eva to walk down the staircase. The music was entrancing him. He could hardly breathe.

Finally, it happened. The lady of his dreams. The one and only person that makes his heart leap every time he sees her. His Eva appeared at the top of the stairs. The flowing white satin dress that Linda and Mama created was mystical and magical. She looked like a goddess. Linda and Opal, walking her slowly, methodically down the long stairs, to give her to him. Edgar's pulse beat with each step she took. His breathing stopped for moments without him realizing it. Prizi jabbed him, with an elbow to the ribs, realizing he needed to start breathing again or he would pass out before Eva got to them. He smiled at Prizi to thank him, now realizing one of the reasons why it was so important for others to be standing with him in this moment.

Eva's veil softly covered her face. He could still see her loving smile shining through it. To think that that smile was for him was overwhelming to his heart. To think that they would be spending the rest of their lives together and raising their children together was more than he could handle. He did not know if he would ever be happier in his life than this moment. Knowing that they would be together, it could only get better.

She arrived at the chuppah. The Rabbi spoke words. Edgar was sure he did because his lips were moving. All Edgar could think of was Eva saying, "I do." All Eva could think of was Edgar saying, "I do." Then they heard those words slip easily from each other's mouths and into their hearts.

Everyone in the room could feel the love between them. The vows were exchanged. The glass was shattered. The party began.

The cousins and the quartet began the festivities with lively folk and dance music. Everyone in the reception line greeted each of the guests. The reception was held on the terrace and lasted until the early morning light. When the live musicians needed a break, the phonograph was brought out. The latest records were played. Everyone needed to party and have some fun. The political atmosphere and hard-working community needed a reprieve from the world's atrocities.

Large white candles were sprinkled throughout the festive rooms and terrace. They twinkled like the milky way. The terrace was as elegantly adorned as the magnificent foyer. Music, dancing, feasting, and laughter went on for hours. Some heated political conversations did pop up. More wine was poured and several evil looks from spouses squashed those conversations.

Everyone was thrilled for the new couple. Friends, family, and neighbors were so happy to be there celebrating with them and celebrating with everyone in the village. Almost everyone at the wedding had something to do with the farming and wine industry. They did not get to dress up and party very often. Everyone was reveling in the joyous festivities.

Everything was picture perfect. From the decorations and wedding dress, to every piece of silver, china, and crystal that were brought out to serve the elaborate and delicious meal. The chefs had outdone themselves in every aspect. The ladies that baked the cake made it five tiers, with pink, red, and yellow icing roses draping down every side. When the musicians and phonograph took a break, Eva and Edgar charmed their guests with duets, Eva on flute and Edgar, of course, on his viola.

This was the most joyful night that Tokaj had seen for a long time. The dancing went on until the wee hours in the morning. There was no shortage of wine and food, dancing and partying by young and old. Eva and Edgar said goodbye to the last of the guests at about four o'clock in the morning. The most wonderous, memorable night had been had by all.

Chapter Twelve

The Honeymoon

Music: "Body and Soul" Coleman Hawkins
"Bubbles in the Wine" Lawrence Welk

History: October 9 Hitler issues orders to prepare for the invasion of Netherlands, France, Luxembourg, and Belgium.

The newly announced Mr. and Mrs. Holthaus's honeymoon would be for a week at the small stone guest cottage on the vineyard property. They would use it as their home until they left for Düsseldorf. It was located on the shore of the large, sparkling, blue lake. Sandor and Rita's chalet was located farther down the same lane. The vineyard staff had surprised the couple with decorating the cottage with the same decorations used for the wedding. Ropes of roses, grapevines, candles and evergreens tied with twine, were everywhere. The sweet aroma filled the air.

At the end of the reception, at about four o'clock in the morning, when Edgar and Eva were saying their goodbyes to their family and friends, the sparkling horse-drawn covered carriage was waiting for them just outside the terrace. Sandor was driving the gorgeously adorned carriage. Rocky was one of the two horses carrying them to their cottage. He and the other gorgeous horse were decked out in full regalia and jingle bells. Linda made sure Rocky got to be one of the horses to carry them. She knew how much Eva loved him and would appreciate seeing him. He had to be a part of the wedding.

Edgar picked up Eva and swooshed her off her feet. She giggled with surprise and excitement. He gently sat her down on the leather-covered carriage seat. Then, like a man struck by cupid, dazed with delight, sat down beside her.

With a "giddy-up" and a tap of the whip on the lead horse's hindquarters, Sandor carried them away to the little stone cottage which had been used for honeymooners for generations.

The newlyweds blissfully looked deep into each other's eyes as they were carried away. No words were needed. They were the happiest couple on earth.

The clippity-clop of the horse's hooves pounded on the hard dirt road. The couple was at peace in each other's arms.

Edgar broke the silence. He spoke the first words that he would speak to her when they were finally alone as a married couple: "Mrs. Holthaus, I'm so humbled to be your husband. I will serve you for the rest of my life," he said with deep sincerity.

Eva teared up and replied, "I am so grateful and honored to be your wife, Mr. Holthaus. I will serve and love you for the rest of our lives."

They leaned into each other's arms, held each other tight, and kissed a kiss that tasted like honey and Azur wine.

Sitting back on the large leather seat that enveloped them, they held each other tight like they were never going to let go.

The ride was a bit bumpy on the old farm dirt road. They did not even notice. It did not take too long to get to the cottage. Sandor reined in the horses and stopped in front of the moonlit cabin. The reflection of the moon danced off the lake that was just outside the back porch of the tiny bungalow. Sandor announced their arrival as if he were carrying royalty. In his eyes, he was. He assisted with the bags while Edgar picked up Eva to carry her over the threshold. Sandor wished them his best, hugged them both, then left into the dark of the night with the horses and carriage.

The warmth and light from the fireplace were inviting them in. The fire had been lit by two of the cousins just prior to their arrival. Peter and Padraig had run about half an hour ahead of the carriage to make sure the fire was lit. The evergreen and roses filled the cabin with a luscious smell that was enticing them in.

While Edgar was carrying Eva across the threshold, he whispered in her ear, "This night is about you. The rest of my life is about you," Edgar said gently, turning to look deeply into Eva's ice blue, penetrating eyes. He placed her tenderly at the side of their satin-draped bed. Pink and red rose petals had been placed lovingly around the inside of the quaint little cabin and on the bed.

Eva stood quietly looking deeply into his eyes. She knew it was going to be a wonderful night because they genuinely loved each other.

"This night is the night that I want to show you that from this moment forward it is all about you." Edgar stated. "Do you trust me?" Edgar asked, with his loving smile, as he held her closely to him with one hand on the middle of her back and the other on the small of her back.

"Yes, of course, I do. I wouldn't have said 'I do' unless I trusted you," Eva answered with immense sincerity and her perfect little ornery smile that Edgar cherished so much.

The warmth and soft flicker of the fire from the fireplace gave an exquisite, romantic glow to the room.

Eva stood in her well-danced-in wedding gown facing Edgar on the side of their honeymoon bed. He took off his top hat and tails and placed them on the chair behind him. He placed a stack of records on the phonograph that he had chosen weeks ago.

Edgar had borrowed the phonograph from the main house to have in the cabin during the week of their honeymoon. He had borrowed some soft instrumental music - Bing Crosby, Cole Porter, and Duke Ellington - for dancing and making love to. He brought a radio to enjoy some Hungarian music also.

Edgar had prepared some words deep from his heart for this moment. He wanted Eva to feel comfortable with their first time together. He wanted it to be the most memorable night of their lives.

He began by unbuttoning the ten, satin-covered buttons that were on each of the cuffs of her sleeves. As he slowly unbuttoned each button, he kept his eyes completely locked into Eva's dazzling eyes. He could never get enough of looking into them.

He began his well-rehearsed promises to her. "You are my rosebud." Edgar paused to let that sink into Eva's heart. "I hope that I can help you bloom into the rose that you have given me to treasure. I will tend to you and honor you all our lives. Anything you need, I will do my best to get for you. When we are young and healthy, we will grow together to capture our dreams," Edgar said with deepest sincerity in his voice.

He finished unbuttoning her right sleeve and continued to unbutton her left sleeve, taking his time to slowly appreciate every moment. Eva was loving every word that flowed from his luscious lips. She wanted these moments to last so she could remember them their entire lives.

"When we are old, we will enjoy the memories that we made and the family that we have created," he continued.

"I promise you, you are mine and mine alone. My eyes are for you and only you. There is no one in this world that I could cast my eyes upon that would be equal to your beauty, inside and out. The beauty that comes from deep within your heart has captured mine. You have snared me with your whole heart. I am your captivated slave and warrior."

Eva's eyes started to brim with tears of deep joy. She had never heard anything like these words before. She did not realize how romantic Edgar was.

Edgar took off his shirt to wipe her tears away. His bare, strong, tanned chest revealed to her. Her knees buckled at his handsome physique. His hard work on the vineyard had him looking muscular and absolutely tantalizing. She wanted to touch every rippling muscle and kiss every inch of his amorous body. To taste his skin on her tongue. To swallow his taste in her mouth. She was beginning to feel heat in places she had never felt heat before.

He stood closer to her. Wrapped his strong arms around her. Drew her into him as if they were one, for a deep long sensual kiss, his bare chest pressing up against her breasts. Her wedding dress was still on. They could feel their heartbeats become one even through the dress.

"Feel my heart?" Edgar whispered into her ear. "It beats for you."

Eva nodded her head yes and rested herself into his muscular chest, knowing she was fully loved. She could hear the pounding of his heart.

"You own this heart. It is yours. My sweetheart, my rosebud, turn around," Edgar slowly turned her as if they were dancing. She faced their bed. A row of thirty-five satin covered buttons that draped down her firm gentle back, were waiting Edgar's careful touch.

Eva said nothing. She turned, by the touch of his hands, in the mystical dance that she was experiencing. She awaited the next gentle words from her lover.

"My rosebud, I have loved you from the moment that I first saw you. My hope is that you open to me day by day as a rose opens to her devoted gardener. I am your devoted gardener. My highest purpose in living is to look after you and tend to you." Edgar continued to pour out his promises. He wanted Eva to know all that he had been holding in his heart from the very first day they met.

Words would not be enough. Making love to his beloved was going to open a whole new world for them. He wanted her to blossom to her very fullest potential in every way. He would be her gardener. She would always be his intriguing, beguiling love, his sweetheart, his rosebud.

After their slow twirl, Eva faced their honeymoon bed. He pulled her into him with his powerful arms. He held her firmly into his body. They swayed to the beat of their own music. They both heard it. It was like they had known each other from past lives.

He lifted her thick, black, long curls off her neck. She tilted her neck to the right where he had gently placed her long luxurious curls. He placed his soft sensual lips on her neck and began to kiss every inch and then down her spine until he reached the top of her wedding dress with his kisses. It gave her goosebumps all over her body. He was touching places that had never been touched before. Not like that.

He began to unbutton the long line of buttons that embraced her voluptuous body, all the way down to the small of her back. One by one he gently unbuttoned each one, then kissed her back after each one was undone. Soft music was playing in the background. The fire was not the hottest thing in the room. The heat between their bodies was moving her to melt into his embrace. They were both entering a new world that they were very much wanting to be in.

With every button that was unbuttoned came a new promise from Edgar and a kiss where the button lay.

I love you because of the shine in your eyes that take me to the sun and feel its heat.

I love you for the smile that grips my heart every time I see it across your lovely face.

I love you for your hair that drapes down across your shoulders to the small of your back. I could lose myself forever in it.

I love you for your ears that hear every word I say and consider them to be important.

I love your mind. It's thoughtful and kind and open to learn about the richness that the world has in it.

I love you for your skin so precious and sensual to touch.

I love you for your shoulders how they are so soft and lean into me when we you want to enfold yourself into me in sorrow and in loving moments.

I love your arms how they wrap around me and how they reach out to help others.

I love your hands. They are tender and soft but with some callouses from hard work and the aptitude to play music and paint beautiful art. And when they touch me, it makes me feel like I am in the presence of an angel.

I love your breasts. They make my blood rise with their beauty and amorous beauty. Your nipples grow hard at my touch. I cannot and will never get enough of them.

I love your back. It's strong and sleek and it bends into me when I press you close to me.

I love your womb. It will carry our children. It will bear our love to the world.

I love your legs. The way they take you on a run thru the woods.

The way they wrap around me when we are wrapped together in sweet embrace.

The way they take authority on Rocky when you ride him through the vineyards.

I love your precious lovely fire, the center of your sexual desire,

The beautiful flower that you have allowed me to have as a gift for the rest of my life. I will treasure your clitoris as a fragile gift that I will learn about every time that I touch it and give my all to it.

The last button was undone. The dress fell to the floor. In the dance that they had started an hour ago they were about to take to an even higher level of sensuality. She turned to face him. He held her at her waist. Picked her up as if she were a fragile porcelain doll. Gently laid her down on the satin covers.

Eva began to unbutton her lover's tuxedo pants. They dropped to the ground. He carefully took off her lace undergarments piece by piece, delicately, slowly, kissing every area that he uncovered, licking, tasting her as he went down.

She could barely breathe. He loved it. She was full of love. Her eyes were shut. She had never experienced such deep, hot lovemaking. He grabbed her by the waist again. This time he was more forceful. He playfully threw her up to the top of the large, four-poster, king-size bed. He chased after her as she fell into the soft pillows. He fell into the pillows beside her. They kissed long and lovingly. He placed her hand on his penis. It was rock hard. It felt hot in her hand.

"This is what you do to me," Edgar embraced her with overwhelming passion.

Eva took his hand to her breasts. Her nipples were hard. He reached down to slowly kiss, lick, and taste them.

"This is what you do to me," she said back to him.

She wanted him to know that she was feeling things that she had never felt before. She took his hand and placed it where she was feeling a driving, pumping heat that she knew only he could have brought to her, only he could satisfy.

For hours they explored, enticed, learned about each other, loved, caressed, tasted, touched, and embraced this new world that they were so fortunate to have been given.

Eva had orgasm after orgasm while Edgar tempted her with all that he had to offer. Their lovemaking was hot and insatiable. They were one. They had never been more fulfilled and completely satisfied.

The exhausted couple woke up late that morning, almost noon. They found a basket of goodies on the front porch. Freshly baked muffins, homemade jams, butter, and teas someone had lovingly gifted to them. They made themselves breakfast. Enjoying their breakfast on the back porch looking out over the picturesque lake, they decided to go skinny-dipping. Covered with only towels, they raced down to the shore and jumped in. There was no one around. It was their own little world. It was a little cold at first. They did not care. They were having the time of their lives, laughing at themselves at how far they had come in such a short amount of time.

Eva splashed water at Edgar. He splashed back. His handsome, deep laugh made her want more of him. He swam to her to capture her up in his arms. He threw her as far as he could throw her. She giggled all the way until she went under water. She swam under water to him. She reached out to find that he was already hard. She loved that she made him that way. Her lips wrapped around his rock-hard penis. She licked and sucked him until she ran out of breath. He was loving her touch. She bounded up above the water, quickly catching her breath. They kissed, played, and made sweet love in the water. They were having so much fun loving each other. They did not notice the yelling coming from the road until they got closer to shore.

"This is a dream. Are we really married? Didn't I just fall on your painting yesterday?" Edgar joked.

"Yes, and I will always be mad at you for that," Eva laughed.

"But didn't it turn out great?" Edgar reminded Eva.

"I guess. We'll have to see," she answered with a cute smile as they swam to shore.

There was yelling still coming from the road. Sandor and Rita had been on the road for a while, yelling toward the cottage, trying to get the young couple's attention. Eva and Edgar did not hear yelling until they were near the shore. They ran out of the water, grabbed their towels and each other and ran up to the cabin. They saw Sandor and Rita on the road. Sandor was driving the tractor. Rita was sitting on the fender.

Eva went inside the cabin to get dressed. Edgar tied the towel around his waist and ran to the tractor to see what they wanted. It had to be important for them to be interrupting their honeymoon. He hoped no one was sick or hurt.

"What's going on?" Edgar asked loudly so he could be heard above the rumble of the diesel engine.

"It's started, my friend. It's started," Sandor said with tears coming to his eyes, trying to catch his breath from being worn out from anxiety.

Edgar looked at him with an overwhelming wonder of what he could possibly be talking about. He turned to Rita who was also overwhelmed, trying to hold back tears. Edgar had never seen Sandor crying before.

"What's started?" Edgar asked with some fear in his voice. He could not imagine what was making them so frightened.

"The war, my son," Sandor said with great despair, "Hitler bombed Poland this morning. We just got word. We're meeting at the house. Get down there as soon as possible," Sandor ordered, with his voice cracking.

Sandor and Rita took off toward the mansion. Edgar ran to the cottage to get Eva.

Chapter Thirteen

Decisions

Music: "My Prayer" Ink Spots
"You Are My Sunshine" Jimmie Davis, Charles Mitchell

History: The German cruiser "Deutschland" seizes the American freighter *SS City of Flint* and its crew, accusing them of contraband. Led by a prize crew the ship is ordered to go to Germany, causing a diplomatic occurrence with the United States and stirring American public opinion.

Edgar's mind was going in every direction after hearing this news. He ran to the cabin to let Eva know what was going on. She had already seen the looks on Sandor and Rita's faces. She had no idea what they could be that concerned about. She had gotten dressed in her bib overalls and work boots. She felt as if they needed to follow Sandor and Rita wherever they were going.

Edgar entered the cabin and saw that Eva had the intuition to get dressed in work clothes, "Oh good, you're so smart," he spoke in admiration. "I need to get changed into work clothes too" Edgar said frantically, trying to tell her without scaring her too much.

"What's going on?" Eva asked as she helped Edgar find his work clothes.

He threw everything on as fast as possible. He was trying to catch his breath and think quickly on what they needed to do as a couple. This would bring a huge change to their plans. He sat down on the bed to tie his boots.

Eva waited patiently for him to catch his breath and his thoughts to tell her what was going on. She could not imagine what she was about to hear.

Edgar finished tying his boots. He stood and took her in his arm. "It's bad, Eva." He hugged her as tight as he possibly could.

She waited for him to speak. Being held by him gave her comfort. No matter what it was, she knew they could get through it together. She was trying to be patient. It was killing her to wait for his explanation.

He breathed deeply and said, "Hitler, Germany, has bombed Poland. We will not be safe here for long. We need to make some decisions. World War II has begun. We're meeting at the mansion. You can call Lawrence and Opal, and let them know we are meeting. They need to be there too."

Their perfect world just shattered. In twenty-four hours, they went from their highest highs to their lowest lows.

The couple took off running down the dirt road to the main house. It was about half a mile behind the barnyards.

They came in through the kitchen door at the back of the mansion. The phone was upstairs in the library.

The first person Eva saw when she entered the kitchen was Linda. She ran to her as if she was her mother. In so many ways she was. They hugged like they had never hugged before.

"I've called your Mama and Papa. They should be here any minute," Linda informed her. "They need to be a part of the discussion and plans. They're family. They needed to be involved in plans and be protected too."

"Oh, thank you so much," Eva said, hugging her even tighter.

Eva agreed and was thankful that her grandparents were considered family. They were so wise. They could also offer stability and wisdom at this time.

It was about two o'clock in the afternoon when all the staff and family arrived.

Everyone was seated around the long dining room table. There were so many people that some of the younger ones sat on the floor.

Prizi began, although in his heart he did not know where exactly to begin. "The first thing we need to do is pray. Lawrence, you are the eldest amongst us. Would you honor us with a prayer?"

Lawrence stood and solemnly gave a brief but powerful prayer that comforted and gave everyone peace.

"Thank you so much, Lawrence," Prizi said with much appreciation, "All right, you all know by now that the Nazis have bombed Poland. No matter what your political beliefs are, this I know: We are Jewish, and Hitler hates us. Sandor and Rita, you're not Jewish, but you're family. We have a lot of work to accomplish since taking on the Kovacs' farm," He looked over at his sons, sitting on the floor and asked, "We need about ten of your friends to help us get through this harvest. We need to bring it in faster than ever. Can you boys get ten good workers from amongst your friends that don't have farm work of their own to do?"

Samuel looked at Daniel, Peter, Padraig, and Akos. They all nodded yes.

Eva thought to herself that she could bring Helena and Emily to help. They were both good workers. She raised her hand to ask permission to bring them along. Prizi thought that would be a great idea. He trusted Eva to know if they were good workers.

"All right, then, get them here tomorrow morning. Sandor, what do you think about making some hiding places for safety areas for us in the wine cellars?" Prizi asked.

"Yes, sir, I can do that immediately," Sandor answered with a sigh of relief. He had been wanting to finish the hiding places that he had started. He would add one more in a wine cellar that was closer to the house so they could get there in a hurry if need be.

"Will you need help?" Prizi asked.

"I'll take one of the boys. Akos?" He nodded at Akos to see if he would want to help. Akos nodded back with a yes. "That's all I'll need. Rita can help me too. If we can make the meals simple to make so her and the kitchen crew's work is lighter, it would give her time to help me," Sandor answered.

"Yes, that sounds good," Prizi said. "Linda, what concerns do you have?"

"After the farm and our safety are taken care of, I would like to think about hiding our special memories, valuables, photos," Linda answered.

"Right. Can I leave you in charge of that?" Prizi asked.

"Yes," Linda answered

"Lawrence and Opal, what concerns do you have? Of course, we will make room for you for a hiding place here if need be." Prizi asked.

"Thank you. We can make a place in our wine cellar to hide, unless it doesn't work out to be a good place. We will come here as a second choice," Lawrence answered. "We've hired a man, Al Hartman, to work with us at the butcher shop. You can have Eva full time for the grape harvest. Al is good with horses too. He's been a farrier all his life. If you need his help, I'm sure he would help in any way that you need."

"Thank you, Lawrence. Much appreciated. You know you are always welcome here for anything," Prizi said. "You know that I have disagreed with you and Sandor before on the alliance between Hungary and Germany; however, being Jewish and the fact that Hitler hates Jews, I am certain that we need to plan for any situation."

"Yes, understood," answered Lawrence, like one soldier to another.

"Edgar, Eva, what are your concerns? How do you want to proceed?" Prizi asked.

Edgar looked at Eva to get the nod from her to speak on their behalf. With unspoken understanding, she nodded yes.

"We have an offer on the table in Düsseldorf. We need to get there before it is too unsafe to travel. We also know that you need help. We can stay until the end of October, unless things get worse and we need to leave sooner. I also have an offer on the table in New York from the NYC symphony," Edgar explained.

The offer from NYC caught everyone by surprise. No one knew this. They all gasped. Especially Opal and Lawrence.

"We didn't know you had an offer in New York City," Prizi said.

"We didn't want to spill the beans unless we were going to go," Edgar explained.

"What do your parents think?" Linda asked.

"They are for whatever puts us in the safest situation," Edgar answered.

"Eva, are you all right with New York City?" Prizi asked.

"I am, if it is the right thing to do for our safety," Eva answered.

She looked at Mama and Papa as she said this. There was silence in the room for a few moments. No one knew what to say. Eva was tearing up. Mama and Papa were tearing up. They could not imagine being that far apart from one another.

Then from the silence Papa spoke with conviction in his voice, "We will do what is best for everyone," Papa said with strength in his voice. His courage gave everyone else peace. They knew he and Sandor had been through WWI and survived. His strength helped them have strength.

"We will get through this together," Sandor piped in.

"Yes, we will," Prizi said, in alliance with the veterans he respected so much, "We have a plan then. We will get through this together. No matter what happens, we will be here for each other. I know I've fought with you and sided with Hungary's alliance with Germany. I see it going a very wrong direction for us. We'll take one day at a time and go from there."

"Why don't we go take care of what we need to take care of personally and for our businesses the rest of the afternoon. Then we can all meet at Temple for Shabbat?" Linda suggested.

"That sounds like a great idea, my love. See everyone tonight," Prizi said.

Everyone went their own directions and began to set things up for what lay ahead of them.

Chapter Fourteen

Shabbat

Music: "The Lamp is Low" Tommy Dorsey

History: October 10 - The last of Poland's military surrenders to the Germans.

Mr. and Mrs. Edgar Holthaus would be making their first outing as a couple at Temple for Shabbat services. Taking their time, they walked to the main farmhouse, holding hands and enjoying every moment. They entered the back door into the lower kitchen. Everything was quiet. No one was around. There was food laying around. Dishes. Utensils. Lights were on. Dinner was over. No one was cleaning it up. Everything seemed out of place. There was some faint chatter coming from the upstairs. They walked up the back stairs to the main dining hall where everyone from family, cooks to farmhands, were gathered around the big radio in the parlor. Bulletins and updates from Germany invading Poland were coming in. It was declared that Germany had started WWII. Everyone was speechless, listening intently to every single, solitary word that was broadcast over the Hungarian airwaves, bracing themselves for what to prepare for.

Edgar immediately started thinking about protecting his lovely bride. What should they do? When should they do it?

When the radio program was over, Prizi and Linda decided to celebrate Shabbat at the mansion instead of the Temple. The radio program lasted too long. They would not make it to the Temple on time. Staff and family were invited to stay if they wished to. A peaceful Sabbath ceremony was held with everyone who was present. Prizi and Aunt Linda presided over it.

Candles were lit. Wax dripped down the candles while prayers were more solemnly said than ever. The light from the candles gave them hope. Everything had changed. Everything was the same too.

After the ceremony was over, everyone quietly walked away not saying anything. They did not know what to say. They did not know what to do. How would this affect them? Would Hungary be safe in their alliance with Germany? Would the alliance be unstable and Germany attack Hungary? Would Russia attack? Are the young men going to war?

Mr. and Mrs. Holthaus walked back to their cottage silently, holding hands tightly. So many questions looming.

Chapter Fifteen

Grape Harvest

Music: "An Apple for the Teacher" Bing Crosby & Connee Boswell
"Indian Summer" Tommy Dorsey

History: Germany's navy high commanders suggest to Hitler they need to occupy Norway.

Like lines of well-trained disciplined soldiers, seemingly endless parallel lines of perfectly manicured grapevines seemed to go on forever. Their golden leaves, ripe grapes, and brown stems covered the hills, slopes, meadows, and valleys of the Schwartzes' vineyard and neighboring properties.

Monday morning at daybreak, Prizi, Sandor, and Edgar rode the horses out to survey the enormous task in front of them. The Schwartzes and Kovacs had bordered each other for generations. The Kovacs were extremely close friends. Prizi did not mind helping them get their grape harvest in. They would have done the same for them. The men sat tall in their saddles on the highest point on the mountains between the two vineyards. Overlooking the vast fields below them, they came face to face with the monumental task. They wondered how they would do it on time. It was an overwhelming job to undertake. They would need to be on top of the extra staff at every turn.

Prizi dismounted his horse. The stage of the grapes needed to be tested. He picked some off a vine to taste them.

"They're ready to go," Prizi spoke after tasting a few, "You two are the strongest and most experienced men I know that can get this done. We've got an impossible task ahead of us and a questionable crew to get it done. We better start. Edgar, get the boys and all their friends together. Train the new boys and girls on what they will need to do. Teach them the difference of picking ripe, unripe, and the noble rot grapes. You and Eva are going to oversee them. Let them know that we need them to work as hard as they possibly can. Stay on top of them. There will be no time for slackers or joking around. If they are slacking and fooling around, send them home. Sandor, you know what to do. Keep this farm running and get those shelters built."

"Yes, sir," Edgar answered, with all seriousness. "I'll go round up the crew and Eva right now."

"No problem, Prizi," Sandor said, reassuring him. "We'll get through this."

"Well, Sandor, if anyone knows, it's you. You have gotten this farm through a couple of generations of problems. I fear this is going to be the hardest yet. I trust you, brother. I appreciate your hard work and dedication," Prizi said, patting his oldest friend on the back as they both turned to ride back to the barn.

Sandor and Akos would be starting in the blacksmith shop this morning. Their job was to keep machinery running, livestock healthy, and get the hiding places built.

Samuel, Daniel, Peter, Padraig, and their ten friends gathered at the top of the barnyard area. Helena and Emily were there too. Everyone eager to help. The girls were eager to show they could out work the boys. The green crew was waiting for instructions and guidance from Edgar and Eva. Edgar and Eva came around the corner on a tractor pulling a wagon. The wagon was full of large, woven, grape-gathering baskets. They brought extra gloves in case someone did not bring any. Canteens of water were on the wagon too.

The tractor and wagon pulled up in front of the crew. Eva jumped off the fender of the tractor. Edgar turned off the loud engine so the crew could hear him.

"Okay, ladies and gentlemen," Edgar began with a serious tone. "There will be no messing around. We have two farms to harvest in the next two months. Here's how we are going to do it. We will teach you how to do the delicate process of harvesting the grapes. My cousins will help you along with the process when we get out into the vineyards, in case you get stuck. We will weigh every basket that you harvest. Eva, you will keep track of these weights. She will also be watching for quality too. Don't just throw anything in your baskets, or the basket will be disqualified. We want a quality harvest. Whoever has the most harvested at the end of the harvest will win a basket of prizes and a money bonus." Edgar explained. "The competition will keep you on your feet. The speed will help us get through this overwhelming task of harvesting two farms. Agreed?" Edgar asked with a drill sergeant voice.

An overwhelming cheer of acceptance went up from the workers.

"Ok, it starts now," Edgar shot the traditional gun to start the harvest and scare away the evil spirits. "Jump on the wagon. We will take you out to the fields."

Eva jumped back on the tractor fender. Edgar checked each person to see if they had gloves, hats, and proper work clothes for the day. He was happy that everyone was prepared. Rita had packed sack lunches for everyone too.

When workers arrived at the first field, Edgar took the time to show the new ones the difference between the grapes and how to sort them properly. Everyone grabbed their baskets from the wagon. They began at a frantic competitive pace. They stayed at that pace until the harvest was finished at the end of October. Eva kept record of the weights and harvested right along with them. Edgar harvested just as fast as the best of the workers and kept everyone at a challenging pace. He was strict but had a great sense of humor to go along with his strictness. Eva was impressed at how he handled everyone and the harvest. He was the hardest worker she had ever seen. The most handsome too. She tried to keep up the best she could.

Eva was thankful to have Helena and Emily helping. She wanted them to be a part of her life in any way they could. She missed them dearly. They kept up with the pace of harvesting with everyone else.

Edgar saw that everyone was taking the harvest very seriously. They were pushing themselves to the absolute maximum. Every harvest there must be a little levity. The workers had to release and have a bit of fun too. The long afternoons would be sprinkled with jokes and singing by all the workers. Some drinking of wine went along with that. Edgar let them have their fun. He was not as rigid a taskmaster as he let on to be. Unless the work was not getting done. Then he would have sent home the first one that was slacking.

Helena was getting cozy with Samuel. Emily was warming up to Daniel. Edgar and Eva were noticing this and liking it very much. There may be a couple of weddings to go to if this kept up.

Days turned into weeks. Weeks turned into two months. In no time at all the harvest was getting done. The last day of harvest for Edgar and Eva was coming to an end. The harvest moon was going to be out all weekend, the last weekend of the month. It would be a race to the end to see who the winner was of the most grapes harvested. All the workers were pushing hard to the end. Everyone wanted to win. It was going to be an awfully close call. Eva had tallied the results every night and posted them on the wall in the barn. Peter and Padraig were the leaders at this point. The final day would come down to just a few baskets.

Eva and Edgar wanted to award everyone on the last day. They had a huge spread of wine, breads, and cheeses on the terrace at the end of the day on Sunday. This would also be their going-away party to say goodbye to everyone.

"Gather around, gather around," Edgar shouted over the very enthusiastic laborers who were gathered on the terrace.

Prizi, Linda, Mama, and Papa and all the vineyard staff were there to celebrate with the wonderful crew. The Kovac family was there too so they could say thanks to everyone.

"Eva, my beautiful wife, has kept meticulous records of how many pounds of grapes have been harvested. The person that has harvested the most grapes is…." Edgar paused for effect.

"Come on, cousin. Don't keep us in suspense any longer," Samuel laughed.

"Well, it's not you. You ate more than you picked," Edgar said with a hearty laugh.

Everyone broke out in great laughter.

"I will let my beautiful wife make the announcement," Edgar proudly stated and gave the floor to Eva.

"Before announcing the winner," Eva said with a humorous hesitation, "I would like to ask if there are any other announcements that need to be made." Eva looked right at Helena and Samuel. They both blushed with excitement and embarrassment. She loved putting them on the spot. She knew everyone would be excited for their announcement, whether they were ready to announce it or not. She knew her best friend well enough that she wanted to burst at the seams and announce it to the world.

"Well…," Samuel said with a bit of a shy stutter, which was not like Samuel at all.

Prizi and Linda were shocked that he was in such a state. They wanted to laugh. They knew they better not. They did not know what the announcement was, but they had a good idea. They did not want to spoil it for him.

Samuel put his arm around Helena's waist and drew her close to him. She looked like a shining star. She was glowing so much. Eva and Edgar were thrilled for the two of them.

"I have asked this beautiful lady to marry me," Samuel announced, "and, remarkably, she said yes!"

Everyone cheered and screamed with excitement. They could not believe they had kept it a secret. Impromptu dancing and clapping broke out. Prizi, Linda, Sandor, and Rita were in tears and dancing right along with everyone else.

"Congratulations, son and new daughter-in-law," Prizi said as he and Linda hugged them. "We couldn't be happier to have you in our family."

"Thank you," Helena answered with great appreciation to her new in-laws.

"Thank you, Father and Mother. She is my one and only. I can't believe I found her in the vineyard," Samuel said with a mutual laugh with Helena and his parents.

"We love you already, Helena," Linda said with a huge hug to her new daughter-in-law, "Have you set a date?"

"No, we haven't gotten that far. We're in no hurry," Helena answered.

"Just let us know what you need. We will all be there for you," Linda said, with Prizi nodding in agreement.

The dancing and cheering settled down. Eva jumped up on a chair to get everyone's attention, "All right, now to announce the winner…," she stated triumphantly, "The winner of the most grapes harvested by weight on both the Schwartz and Kovac farms is… drum roll please…." Everyone pounded something to make a drum roll.

"It's Akos!"

Everyone broke out in huge laughter. Akos had not been in any of the fields. Akos took the limelight with great prestige. He boldly hopped onto one of the large, long benches, stuck his thumbs in his suspenders and strutted down the bench like he owned the world. He got to the end of the bench and hopped off. Went to Eva and held his hands out as if he were going to get the prizes from her. Eva just smacked him on the bottom and he scooted away with a huge smile. Laughter rang out from everyone.

"All right, enough messing around," Eva said with lightheartedness. "All of you did an amazing job. Everyone worked so hard. We are all thankful to each of you. Our winner is… Padraig!"

The family and staff went wild with hooting and yelling with congratulations to Padraig. He walked up to Eva and Edgar to receive his prizes. They handed him the basket of awards and the envelope of money that was contributed to by Prizi, Linda, and the Kovac family.

"Thank you so very much," Padraig said with humility, which they had never seen before. "I will have to split this with Peter. I know he was close to my total."

"Yes, he was very close all the way through the season," Eva agreed.

Peter thanked him for the acknowledgement. Prizi and Linda hugged them both.

"Daniel, you came in right behind the twins. Congrats! You and Peter get a bottle of our greatest and oldest Azur wine for all of your hard work," Eva announced. "Maybe you could split that with Emily," Eva said, with a wink.

Daniel and Emily turned bright red. Prizi and Linda turned to look at them with lots of questions. Linda turned to Prizi and asked, "What was going on in that vineyard?"

Prizi said, "I don't know, but I like it."

Dancing, feasting, and celebration went on under the full moon for hours. Harvest was over. Wine-making process was in high gear for both vineyards. Eva and Edgar were having a great send-off party. They would take the train to Düsseldorf in two days. Tuesday would be the beginning of their new life away from this loving family.

The party ended at around one o'clock in the morning. It was chilly away from the bonfire that was just outside of the terrace. Edgar and Eva grabbed a quilt to share on the way back to their cabin. They walked by row after row of harvested grapevines. Under the moonlight they could see the end results of all the hard work they and the others had done. They were tired and grateful. They kissed under the stars and made pure sweet love when they got back to their newlywed cabin.

Chapter Sixteen

Tuesday Morning Train

Music: "We'll Meet Again" Vera Lynn

"I'll Remember" Bert Androse and his Orchestra

History: British Prime Minister Chamberlain formally declines Hitler's peace offer in a speech held in the House of Commons.

Tears. How could tears not flow?

Mama and Papa were losing the last of their little family. None of them knew when they would see each other again. Or if they would.

Edgar had given all their bags to the train's porter. The morning fog made it even more gloomy than it needed to be. Mama could not let go of Eva's hand. Papa was a tough old bird. This was bringing him to his knees.

Edgar knew it was the right move to make to keep them safe. He felt somewhat guilty for taking Eva away from the only family she had ever known. He promised to make it up to her in every way.

The boarding whistle blew. The conductor announced loudly for all passengers to board the train, "All aboard!"

Mama gave Eva and Edgar one last kiss on their cheeks. Papa grabbed Eva and hugged her tight enough that the hug would last until they see each other again. He and Edgar shook hands.

"Take care of her every need, Son," Papa lovingly demanded of Edgar.

"Yes, sir, I will," Edgar promised.

The train ride would be about fifteen hours, with a layover at the Vienna station. They decided to go through this route to avoid the danger of layover in Munich.

Mama had made them a thick flannel quilt for a wedding present. They took that out and covered themselves to keep warm on the ride. They slept for a few hours. It was too foggy to see any of the countryside. They were still tired from the heavy work during harvest. It was nice to relax in each other's arms. They wanted to be wide awake when they reached Düsseldorf. They napped on and off. The swaying motion of the train was rocking them to sleep under the warm quilt.

"We have an hour layover in Vienna. Do you want to walk around for a bit to see some sites?" Eva asked.

"That would nice. Vienna is a gorgeous city," Edgar responded as he snuggled up closer to her under their comfy cover.

"You've been there before?" Eva asked.

"I've played in the Great Hall many times." Edgar answered humbly.

"What's the Great Hall?" Eva asked, feeling very out of touch with famous big city sites.

"If we have time, we'll try to see it," Edgar answered.

"I'd love that. I want to go everywhere you have ever been, and I want to see everything that means a lot to you."

"We have a lifetime together. I'm hoping that will happen for both of us."

They snuggled and fell asleep until they got close to Vienna. The conductor's announcement of the train schedule and layover woke them up. Yawning and waking up to the sites of Austria passing by their window was spellbinding for Eva. Edgar sat back and watched her amazement of the beauty of this snow-covered, grand country.

The clacking of the wheels and screeching of the brakes told them that the train depot was near. The train came to a gentle stop. Edgar sees Nazi soldiers right outside their window. He freezes, not knowing what to do. Eva sees them too.

"What should we do?" Eva asks.

"Whatever we do, let me do the talking. Your broken German will give you away. They will hear your Hungarian accent, and we could be searched or taken away to somewhere we do not want to be," Edgar strongly advised.

Eva nodded, stopping her talking that instant.

The Nazi soldiers passed by their train. They did not get on. Edgar and Eva let out a sigh of relief.

"We need to change trains as fast as possible. Our sightseeing just ended," Edgar explained. "I've changed trains here before. Let me ask one of the porters the quickest way to get to our next train. We don't want to run to it. That would draw attention to us."

"Right," Eva agreed.

"I'll be right back," Edgar promised.

He headed to the porter that was coming through their car. The porter looked nervous and pale with fright. Edgar approached him cautiously.

"Could you tell me the fastest way to get to the train to Düsseldorf?" Edgar spoke frankly hoping for a quick response.

"You see that platform over there?" The porter asked, pointing out the window to the platform across two other tracks.

"Yes," Edgar answered.

"Go there, hurry. The SS are near." The porter kept walking.

Edgar nodded to Eva. She sprang up so they could move quickly and as inconspicuously as possible. They gathered their luggage and walked briskly and cautiously to the next platform. Eva pulled the quilt over her head like a hood to stay warm and to not let her long black hair be seen by the Nazi's. She was not blonde like Edgar. Her features would stand out and put them in danger.

They boarded the train to Düsseldorf as quickly as possible. They found seats toward the back of the car to stay out of everyone's sight. Their hearts were pounding through their chests. They hoped the train would leave before any Nazis boarded.

The sound of the engine started its roar. The movement of the cars on the track was like music to their ears. The chug, chug, chug allowed them to breathe.

The train was packed. Eva and Edgar wondered where all the people were going. Many fearful faces. Many empty, lost eyes. They stayed to themselves. This was not a pleasure trip for these travellers. Most of the passengers looked terrified. They wrapped themselves up under the quilt again and fell asleep until they got to Munich.

When the train was approaching Munich, the conductor announced their arrival. His loud, deep voice woke them. They would stay on the same train and in their same seats this time. Looking out the window did not seem as pleasant as it was before their stop in Vienna.

Looking out the window at the Munich stop, they saw more German soldiers than had been in Vienna. Suddenly, several of the Nazis boarded their train car. They passed by every seat as if going through a barracks inspection. Eva stayed completely quiet, hoping they did not say anything to them. One of them asked for Edgar's papers. Edgar pulled out his papers and Eva's. The officer, who looked younger than Edgar, stared at Eva for what seemed like forever. She was afraid to her core. She could feel herself going cold, afraid she was going to go into shock and faint, leaning harder into Edgar to have his body hold her up. He felt her fear as she leaned in for support. She knew it would be dangerous to show fear.

"Breathe... breathe," she silently told herself.

Eva made sure her hair was fully covered with a scarf to protect her from being recognized as a Jew again. She did not make eye contact with the Nazi. Edgar would speak for her. The soldier took his whip and snapped it at her forehead, pushing her scarf back to reveal her thick black hair. Edgar wanted to beat him, take him down, and shove the whip where he would never see it again. Wisdom and well-understood restraint stopped him in his tracks. The soldier looked at Eva in the eyes and gave a threatening grunt to her. She stood firm as a rock on the outside, dying on the inside, hoping this moment would pass as soon as possible. The train needed to start rolling quickly away from this horrific man. Disgruntled, the soldier snapped back into alignment with all the other soldiers. He must have been the one in charge. He marched all of them off the train. It left an indelible mark on Eva and Edgar. They would be sharper and more on their toes should anything like this ever happen again.

Eva thought she may have to lighten her hair or wear light makeup when traveling. She never wanted to be picked out of a crowd again. The stern stomping of the Nazis' unison military pounding steps passed by them and exited the train. Edgar and Eva were relieved beyond words. Their next stop was Düsseldorf. They just needed to make it to his parents' home. It was walking distance to the train station.

Chapter Seventeen
Düsseldorf

Music: "Darn That Dream" Mildred Bailey

"Address Unknown" Ink Spots

History: October 12: Adolf Eichmann begins to deport Jews from Austria and Czechoslovakia into Poland.

The train engine began its welcome rumble. The whistle blew. The announcement that the next stop was Düsseldorf was welcome as rain to Edgar and Eva's ears. They cuddled up under the quilt again. The quilt still felt like a piece of home to Eva. She was getting afraid and homesick. She would dare not tell Edgar. She did not want him to worry about her feeling this way. They were doing the right thing. She saw that now more than ever. She would find her courage to get through this transition. She curled into his strong embracing arms and slept. Edgar slept, this time with one eye open.

Finally, the word they wanted to hear announced the most.

"Düsseldorf," announced the conductor.

Edgar was ecstatic to hear the name of his hometown. Their safety, as temporary as it may be, was just around the corner.

Eva looked out the window to see her new home. It was better than she imagined. It was a brilliant city with lovely buildings. It was spectacular. She also looked to see if there were any soldiers hovering around. None currently. She helped Edgar with their luggage. They would walk just a few blocks, and she would be meeting his parents. She was excited and nervous.

"You'll be fine," Edgar said. "They already love you. Not as much as I love you. How could that ever happen?"

That brought a huge smile to Eva's face. She knew she would love them too. They had to be fantastic to have raised such a perfect person as Edgar.

The couple walked off the platform only to be greeted by Edgar's parents. They had brought Edgar's little wooden wagon, from when he was a child, to help carry their belongings.

"Mother, Father!" Edgar grabbed Eva's hand and ran toward them, "I had no idea you were meeting us."

"How could we not?" Mother said, "We've missed you terribly and we wanted to meet our new daughter as soon as possible."

Eva took note that she said daughter instead of daughter-in-law. Either would have been appropriate. "Daughter" sounded so much better. Mrs. Holthaus immediately reminded her of Linda. Eva had this warm feeling that they would get along wonderfully.

"We need to get home quickly," Father interrupted, with the reality of the situation in Düsseldorf. "There are Nazi soldiers at every turn. We avoid them at all costs."

"But we need hugs first," Mother said with such happiness in her voice.

After hugs and kisses were generously given out, the four of them walked back to the modest three-bedroom row house. Edgar's sister, Lou, was off at college in Spain. It was safer for her to be there.

"You left a boy. You came back a man," Father spoke as they walked. "She's beautiful inside and out. We can tell. We're so happy for both of you. This is a rough time to have a new relationship. You'll be all right though. You'll have each other."

"Thank you, Father. How have you and Mother been? It's so good to be back home," Edgar asked, while pulling his little wagon full of luggage and watching his new bride walk in front of him hand-in-hand with his mother.

"We've been good, worried about you, Eva, and your sister. But we've been good," Father answered. "We've been watching the political situation develop. It's getting heated more than any of us would have expected, going differently, more hateful directions than any of us would have expected."

"We just had a run in in Munich where some soldiers boarded the train, looked at our paperwork. Then one of them took his whip and snapped it in Eva's face. Then, pushed back her hair to see what color her hair was."

Momma stopped in her tracks and held Eva's hand even tighter. "What?"

"What?" Father exclaimed. "I'm sure you wanted to fight all of them. What did you do?"

"It took everything in me to stop from going for his throat," Edgar explained. "I knew we would be in even more danger, and they might separate us if I did anything. We were both like statues, standing as still as we could until they left the car."

"He was very wise and brave," Eva said.

The four of them had come to a complete stop to hear about the incident. It was too dangerous to linger as a group.

"Let's hurry home," Father said, to move them along.

"You must be tired? Hungry?" Mother asked.

"Both," Edgar answered with a laugh.

"Good. I've made your favorite dish, sauerbraten. For dessert, your favorite, apple strudel," Mother answered with great delight.

"Thank you, Mother. I can almost taste it now. I have missed you all so much," Edgar said, wiping away a tear.

"You mean you have missed your mother's cooking," Father laughed.

"Of course. I've missed that more than your cooking," Edgar jabbed back with love.

They reached the door of their home. The lovely smell of his favorite meal and dessert reached him before he reached for the doorknob. He breathed it in as if to breathe home, love and safety into his lungs. Edgar would usually see many neighbors outside or hanging out their windows. Many times, on his return, the neighbors would gather at their home to get the latest news of his travels. It was an eerie feeling coming home to a desolate street. They entered their home and felt a bit of relief. Edgar and Eva knew that from now on they would need to always be on guard.

"Sorry about no one being here to greet you, son. Everyone stays to themselves right now for safety. You will have to do that too. Especially with Eva by your side. Careful who you talk with and where you go," Father explained downheartedly.

"We will," Edgar answered with understanding. "Will you be able to come see me play?"

"Depends on the day, Son. We're trying to figure this new life out as we go. This new regime is anti-Semitic like none we have ever seen in our lifetime," Father explained. "You are half German and can pass as German with your looks and your name. You are also Jewish. They will find you out too."

"Yes, sir. We understand," Edgar answered, shaking his head in agreement.

The newly acquainted family enjoyed their meal and conversation until late into the evening. Once they were all exhausted enough to go to bed, they gave in to their need to sleep, promising to continue catching up with more stories in the morning and for as long as they were staying in Düsseldorf.

During dinner, Edgar and Eva explained that they may go to America for safety reasons. Edgar's parents understood. They hated that they felt like they had to leave their home to be safe. They regretfully understood.

The next few weeks were very pleasant and loving for Eva. Mother and Father were completely accepting of her as a daughter. She felt as if she had lived there all her life. Her German was getting better. She could see settling into a nice life in Düsseldorf, if only circumstances were different. She felt safe enough inside their home. A couple calls every week were made to Linda, Prizi, Mama, and Papa to let them know everything that was happening with them and their plans.

Eva wished she could explore the city, symphony, and especially the art museums. Oh, how she missed painting. She brought her easel and some of her supplies. She set them up in the bay window in their bedroom. It faced the small backyard. She painted when she had some alone time. It took her back to her private sanctuary on the Tisza. So much had happened since the last time she painted there. So much has changed. Sometimes tears would roll down her cheeks desiring to go back there in simpler times. Then she would laugh at herself remembering that all she wanted to do was get away on a big adventure and go to Paris or some exotic places to paint. She thought to herself, "I suppose humans are never satisfied."

Edgar went to work almost daily, practicing with the symphony. Most of his old friends were still there. There were some new faces. He was one of the only Jewish members of the symphony. His incredible skills always kept him in the honored first seat position.

David and Timothy, from the horn section, his best friends in the orchestra, warned him of the new dangers that Jews were facing. They had been helping some Jewish families escape through Amsterdam. Edgar asked if they could help him and Eva escape. They absolutely agreed to get them to a safe house in Amsterdam where they could wait for their ship to arrive that would take them to America. No one else could know of this plan. All four of them could be arrested.

Mother and Father Holthaus had said their goodbyes to Edgar and Eva at home. They did not want to cause a disturbance at the train station. The symphony members would have thought it strange if they were crying. They knew they would not be able to stop crying.

The orchestra would travel by train to Amsterdam for their Christmas concert. It was an annual event that the musicians looked forward to. Some spouses would travel on the train with them. For Eva to be traveling with Edgar at this time was not looked upon as something unusual. You never knew what political party your friends or neighbors were siding with. They had to be incredibly careful about who to trust and what they spoke. Eva and Edgar sat near Timothy and David on the train. They always wanted to stay inconspicuous.

Eva and Edgar had not packed much. They could not. They did not want to look as if they were planning on staying or moving on to another destination. She had mailed her easel, flute, and a few important items to the New York City Symphony. Edgar brought an overnight case and his viola to Amsterdam. The Orchestra was only in Amsterdam for three days of performances.

Timothy and David were prone to go to all night parties in Amsterdam, saw their favorite hookers and visited as many bars as they could until dawn. So, no one from the orchestra was suspect when they were gone all night. No one would have thought they were getting Edgar and Eva placed in a safe house before the orchestra left for Düsseldorf the next morning.

Chapter Eighteen

Sweet Low Tones in Amsterdam

Music: "And the Angels Sing" Martha Tilton

"I Didn't Know What Time It Was" Benny Goodman

History: November 23: Polish Jews are ordered to wear Star of David armbands.

One Week Later

The Amsterdam Attic Apartment

In hiding. Waiting for the ship that would take them to America.

This secret safe house / apartment has been used by many refugees attempting to escape Europe. It was on the Nazi's radar as a hiding place for Jews. Those who lived there were considered traitors and spies.

The Düsseldorf Orchestra was back home. Edgar and Eva were now wanted by the SS for being deserters and traitors. Snitches led the SS to the secret apartment.

The movement of the sweet low tones of the viola were suspended in Eva's disoriented mind. Within the fog of lost thoughts and reality, in her mind's eye, she was watching Edgar's fingers play on the strings of his most treasured viola. The reality of the scene directly above her was being held off by perplexity, horror, and denial.

Edgar's warm blood was siphoning slowly through the floorboards of the sparsely furnished concealed apartment. Drip by drip his blood coated Eva, his young bride. Edgar had hurriedly hidden her in the crawl space, that he had devised for the two of them, underneath the floorboards of their newlywed bed.

Time had run out. They had been hunted down by those who were ordered to stalk them down after their disappearance from the last concert.

Gunshots rang out from the two apartments below theirs. They thought they had time to both get hidden. The Nazi soldiers were too fast. They killed the neighbors in the two apartments below them. Then, like savage beasts, burst into their hidden attic quarters.

The murderers had been tipped off by the underground Nazi alliance members in Amsterdam. Edgar only had time to get Eva hidden. His fate was sealed as soon as the terrorizing Nazis crashed through their door. His only hope was that his young bride would survive the attack.

While Eva lay in the fetal position in the frigid, dark, dank crawl space in her secondhand, threadbare, flannel gown she heard her husband beg for his life in his native German. There was no mercy given. The bullets flew like water from a hose from the machine guns. The sound was deafening. His screams cut through her like the sharp edge of a dagger into her heart, tearing her apart.

The soldier's job was half done. They saw no sign of Eva in the one room apartment. The pounding of the soldiers' boots as they turned to leave made dust fall from in between the floorboards and mix with Edgar's blood. The mixture dropped onto Eva's shivering body. There was no warmth left in the blood. Seconds after the SS left the room, the sound of Edgar dragging himself to be near his lover was over her head. He said nothing. He couldn't. He used the last of his strength to cover her hiding area, be near her, to protect her.

Eva understood what he was doing. She did not understand that she was going into shock. Her state of mind was fading in and out of twilight unconsciousness.

When she had some moments of clarity, she tried to think of what to do. From what she could tell there were about six to eight men that had come into the room. They are still looking for her. She needed to stay quiet. It was freezing in the crawl space. Edgar was unconscious and dying slowly above her, if not dead already. Slowly she could feel herself blacking out. She lost control and could not stop her body from collapsing into a dark and twilight state.

Who were these men that they would come searching for a young couple and hunt them down like prey? Some of Edgar's executioners may have even enjoyed hearing him play Wagner in the concert a week ago. Snitches were all over Europe informing the SS of traitors. It became known that Edgar and Eva were Jewish and that they were deserters. The Nazis would not tolerate traitors or runaways. Especially not a national treasure like Edgar. The soldiers were ordered to find and kill them to make a point to all others who were thinking of doing the same thing.

The soldiers had forced their way into the three-family home and killed all its residents. She thought.

Eva's mind continued to flow in and out of consciousness. She was now a wanted criminal by the Nazi party. Her husband was dead. There was no way of getting back home without being noticed. She could not go to Düsseldorf and put her in-laws in danger. How could she go forward to America if Edgar were not with her? She lay there in the freezing hiding place deciding to die. Her morbidly cold body was covered with Edgar's now coagulating blood. His blood had drenched the flannel gown, that was given to her by Teresa, her downstairs neighbor. His life had been poured out to save hers.

The sounds of the soldiers stomping through the apartments and the neighbors' screams had stopped. The sound of silence was enveloping her. Thoughts reeled inside her head making her terrified and panicked. Her mind teemed with out-of-control thoughts and suspicion. The exhaustion finally overtook her. She fell into an almost comatose sleep.

Chapter Nineteen

The Awakening

Music: "I Don't Know" Cripple Clarence Lofton
"Cinderella, Stay in My Arms" Guy Lombardo
History: The British battleship *HMS Nelson* is incapacitated for six months by a magnetic mine left this time by the U-52 off the Loch Ewe.

The sound of someone crying startled Eva out of her haze-like unconsciousness. Had it all been a horrific nightmare? The bitter cold darkness of her encased, tomblike situation told her it had not.

A second later, after hearing the crying, Eva gained her protective senses. She knew instantly that her exhausted mind needed to snap into survival mode. Unaware of how long she had been asleep, she lay there quietly to try to gather clues as to who this was crying above her. It was a soft little voice. Whoever it was, they were sobbing uncontrollably.

Was the person grieving over Edgar? She pondered silently. Maybe it was someone she knew? They had only been here a week. The only people they knew was the young couple, Teresa and Bruce, and their young daughter, Ilse. Was it Ilse? Was she still alive? Someone must have turned Bruce and Teresa in for helping refugees escape. Eva felt overwhelmingly guilty that this little girl was standing over her crying over these deaths.

Unaware of how long she had been asleep, she lay silently, trying to gather herself together to engage with this person without putting herself or the person in grave danger. There may be others in the room.

"Oh, please let it be Ilse. Please let her be alive," Eva thought.

Eva needed to remain guarded while making sure that it was her little neighbor. The flannel gown had been Teresa's. If it was Ilse, she would recognize it. Eva remembered Ilse being sad when her mother gave it to her. It had been like a receiving blanket to her. She had been rocked to sleep in her mother's arms many a night in this nightgown.

Eva searched, by feel in the darkness, almost in vain, to find a measure of the blood-encrusted fabric that was not stained by Edgar's blood. A small stream of light was coming in from a knothole in the floorboard above her chest. The light must have been from a candle that Ilse had brought in. The stream of light allowed Eva to find a clean spot on the gown. It was on the hem. She pulled it up enough to poke a tiny piece of it through the knothole so only Ilse could see it.

Ilse saw it. Recognized it. She gasped and fell backwards in shock, "Eva?""

"Yes, my dear, are you alone?" Eva knew enough English and German to get by in simple conversations.

"Yes," she cried, "all alone." They killed my Mommy and Daddy. Ilse sobbed and dropped to her knees to touch the garment that Eva had pushed through the floorboard.

"Shhhhhh," Eva coaxed, her throat was tightening with fear. "We must be completely silent in case they are close."

"They are gone. I watched them leave in a big truck. I was hiding behind the curtains in my bedroom. I watched them leave."

"Can you help me out of here?" Eva asked her dear little friend, knowing it was going to be an awful task.

"Yes," Ilse said with all the strength she had.

Ilse was afraid to touch Edgar. There was blood all around his body. She knew she had to pull him off the floorboards where Eva was hiding. She mustered the strength, knowing that it was the only way she was going to save Eva.

"I'll push the floorboards up. Can you pull Edgar away from them?" Eva asked.

"Yes," She answered bravely.

Gently, the fearful, newly orphaned child pulled Edgar by his nightshirt and drug his heavy motionless body over just enough to uncover Eva's tomblike encasement.

Eva slowly, agonizingly turned to lay flat on her back. She was frozen. Crusted in place. She needed to use her legs to push the boards up. With a slow hard heave, she busted the boards open that Edgar had so protectively placed himself over. She heard his body move lifelessly away from her.

Her left side had fallen asleep from laying in one position so long. She was stiff, almost immobile. The blood had dried on her, making her look almost mummified. She looked terrifying.

Ilse watched her rise slowly from her hiding space. She gasped and started to cry again.

"Shhhhh," Eva insisted. "We have to be quiet as a mouse."

Ilse understood and hushed herself to protect them both. Ilse reached down to help Eva. She was struggling to move. When Eva finally got out, she saw her lover laying before her, lifeless. She fell on top of him to retrieve any warmth his body might still have in it. Her cries were deep and guttural, almost not humanlike, heaving. She was struggling to keep herself quiet to protect Ilse.

They had to get out of this apartment house. The Nazis could come back at any time.

"We need to leave," said Eva. "I need to get you to a safe place. What do you suggest?"

"My grandparents live around the block," Ilse answered.

"All right, I'll clean up and put on some of Edgar's clothes to make it look like I'm a man. They will be looking for a woman. If we are seen, this might throw them off," Eva explained, "Do you need anything from your apartment?"

"No, I can't go back in there ever again," Ilse started to cry again.

Both girls were sitting on the floor. Both devastated. Eva instinctively grabbed Ilse up in her arms and rocked her in her lap, then looked her in the eyes, "We will get through this." Eva did not know how or when or if they would get through it. She had to tell Ilse this so they could at least try to push through and get through this together.

Eva got up and went into the bathroom to take off the gown and clean up. She hid the gown in the hiding space so no one would detect she had escaped. She threw on Edgar's clothes. Tucked her hair into his hat. They decided to use the back stairwell that led to a dark alley. They would need to stay off the main streets as much as possible. Ilse knew a short cut that would be dark and safer for them to get to her grandparents' tiny, two-bedroom townhouse. She had taken it many times with her mother.

The two exhausted girls ran down the alley as fast as they could. Anyone could turn them into the authorities. No one was safe to trust. They had to run as fast as they could and not stop for anyone or anything.

They reached the grandparents' small fenced in backyard. Some neighborhood dogs were barking. Ilse reached up and tried the gate to see if it was unlocked. Most of the time it would be. She turned the handle and breathed a sigh of relief. It was unlocked. They both ran inside the yard as fast as they could. Now to get the grandparents' attention without waking everyone in the neighborhood. Ilse tapped lightly on the back door. No answer. She tapped a little louder. No answer.

After about ten minutes of waiting in the freezing cold weather, Ilse decided to throw a small rock at their bedroom window that was on the second floor. A light came on. The girls were relieved. Ilse tapped on the door again.

"Who is it?" grumped Grandfather as they heard his heavy footsteps coming down the creaky wooden stairs.

"Grandpa, it's me, Baby," Ilse whispered through the crack between the door and the frame. She had pushed her face up against the window making herself look like a funny little pug dog/ human of some sort.

Grandma heard Ilse's voice and came hurriedly down the stairs. She came down so fast that she was right behind Grandpa when he opened the door.

"What is happening? What's going on?" both grandparents said so fast that they were trampling over each other's words.

"Where's your Momma and Pappa?" Grandpa asked.

Ilse collapsed on the floor. Grandpa picked her up into his arms, then sat her on his lap on the nearest chair. Grandpa and Grandma looked at Eva thinking she was a man. She took off Edgar's hat to reveal that she was a young lady. They did not recognize her. They had never met. Edgar and Eva had kept to themselves to protect themselves and others while in the secret apartment.

Ilse could not speak. All she could do was cry. It was a heaving, deep, guttural cry. Eva sat down on the closest chair, asking permission to sit as she was going down. She was still white as a ghost and having spells of shock just as Ilse was.

"What's the matter, Baby?" Grandma asked gently, understanding they were in severe distress.

Eva knew she had to tell them. Ilse could not speak, "We have come from a terrible situation," Eva began. "My husband and I live upstairs from Ilse. There was an attack from the SS, Nazis in our building. Ilse and I are the only ones that survived. We were hidden."

Grandma and Grandpa began to cry. Grandpa grabbed Grandma with his free arm as she stood next to him. She fell into the chair beside him.

"Is this true? Why would they come to this apartment to kill anyone?" Grandpa asked.

Eva began to cry. "I'm afraid it is my fault. My husband and I escaped from Germany to go to America, and we were hiding until we could get on a ship that is helping refugees."

"It is not your fault, child," Grandma comforted. "It's the Nazis' fault. What is your name?"

"My name is Eva Holthaus." Eva introduced herself to these kind gentle grandparents that reminded her of hers.

"I am Rebecca, and this is Ernest Dekker," Grandma introduced.

"Are they gone?" Grandpa asked.

"Yes, but they are still looking for me. I need to leave as soon as possible. I don't want to put you in any danger," Eva said, with fear and apprehension for their lives.

"They will not find you here. You can stay here as long as you like," Rebecca kindly demanded.

"I'm afraid they might. I believe someone snitched on Teresa and Bruce. They have been brave enough to help hide people," Eva explained apologetically.

"Ernest, what should we do?" Rebecca asked her husband who was still rocking Ilse. She had fallen asleep in his arms.

"Let's get these girls into a safe place. I'll go lay Ilse down in our bed. She can sleep with us tonight. Eva can take a bath. Get her a nightgown. She can sleep in the guest bed. We can't go to the apartment tonight. Let's wait until morning. I'll get some men to help me. We'll take care of things in the morning," Ernest said trying to get a hold of his own grieving, "Does that sound all right to you, Rebecca?"

"Yes. As much as I want to go there right now, I don't want to put any of us in danger," Rebecca answered.

The four settled into their beds. Ilse and Eva slept until late afternoon. Their minds and bodies had been tortured. They were nearly paralyzed with fear. When they woke, they went downstairs to see what time it was and what day it was. Rebecca was sitting at the kitchen table sipping tea. She had a kettle on all day for whoever was passing through her kitchen after such horrible murders. She had had company all day, neighbors, relatives, men helping with the clean-up of the apartments and deaths. She was spent. She was collapsing on the inside but strong on the outside. She had to be for Ilse, Ernest, and their new friend.

Ernest and some male members of the family cleaned the apartments and made arrangements for the undertaker to pick up the bodies. The decision on how Eva wanted to handle Edgar's arrangements were left to her. As much as she did not want to do it, her best choice was cremation. She could take Edgar with her wherever she went. She did not want to bury him in Amsterdam.

Ernest came home. Rebecca could tell he had been through hell. The look in his eyes was like she had never seen before. Ilse rushed to meet him at the door. He scooped her up in his weary arms. He was empty. His heart was shattered into a million pieces. He had seen hell and would forever be changed because of it. Several relatives and neighbors had come over to comfort the family and help with their needs.

Eva had gone back upstairs. She did not want to bring any danger to anyone. She also needed to figure out what her next move was going to be. There was no phone available for her to call home. She wrote a letter to Edgar's parents, Mama, Papa, Linda, and Prizi. She hoped to talk with them before she decided on what to do next. She was stuck in the middle of two worlds. She could not go back to Hungary. It was becoming very unstable. She did not have the talents that Edgar had to get her to America. Would the New York Symphony help her escape Europe?

Chapter Twenty

Where Now?

Music: "Thanks for Everything" Artie Shaw
"White Sails (Beneath a Yellow Moon)" Ozzie Nelson & his Orchestra
History: The Russian invaders begin severe attacks on the Mannerheim line. The Battles of <u>Kollaa</u> and <u>Suomussalmi</u> begin.

The next day was Shabbat. It did not feel like any Shabbat that Eva had ever experienced. Her life was in an unimaginable, spiraling-out-of-control chaos. She had no clear direction. For that matter she did not know if she wanted a direction. She would be just fine to die here with Edgar.

The sun was rising over Amsterdam. The frost on the kitchen windows gave the beams of sunlight a glistening prism effect to the cozy little table area. Ernest was stoking the fire for the day. Rebecca was pouring tea for the four of them. Neighbors had brought over too much food. None of them felt like eating anything. Their grief and mourning were hanging like lead in their hearts.

The funeral for Ilse's parents would be tomorrow. Edgar's remains would arrive in the next few days. She would take him with her wherever she went. Not knowing where she would be going, she had to make the smartest decisions she could for both of them. She wanted to live his dreams for him as much as was humanly possible. Ernest and Rebecca helped her through every step.

Finally, the morning silence was broken by Eva. "I think I need to go to America. I see no other choice. I have written my letters to my family and Edgar's family. I will continue to New York. Does that make sense?" asked Eva of her newfound family, grasping for answers and direction.

"I don't see any other solution," Ernest answered. "We've been pondering it too."

"If you are still on the list for the Nazis to track down, you have no choice," Rebecca agreed. "We will help you. We know a man that deals in trading whiskey from Scotland. We own a bar. We trade and buy with him. He is due to dock any day. He's rough around the edges. Grew up a fisherman. He's a Scottish military veteran. If anyone can get you out of Europe, it's him. His name is Jalvja. Does that sound like something you would be interested in?"

Suddenly, a heavy pounding on the front door jarred them all out of their chairs. Instinctively Ernest knew it was not anyone they knew. It could be the Nazis. Anyone could have given them the location of Eva just to save their own family.

"Rebecca… hide Eva, then come back and sit at the table and don't say a thing," Ernest demanded.

Rebecca took Eva out the back door to the woodshed and quickly shoved her under a pile of wood. She hurriedly came back into the house and sat by Ilse, quickly removing Eva's cup from the table so they would not see that she had been there.

Eva only had a nightgown on. Snow and sawdust were falling on her. Some was falling on her face and into her mouth. She was trying to not cough it out for fear of revealing her hiding place. If the Nazis were there for very long, she would freeze to death. She waited patiently, hoping and praying that her newfound friends would be safe. She was feeling overwhelmingly guilty for what she had brought upon them.

"We are looking for a young lady, a traitor from Düsseldorf. There is information that she may be in this area. What do you know?" asked the large SS officer to Ernest.

Calm and collected, Ernest responds in German, "We have not seen anyone new in the area."

Rebecca is sitting beside Ilse at the table. They were both remarkably calm and quiet. They knew their lives were at stake.

There were three more soldiers that entered the home. Without asking permission, they went through all the rooms and closets in the home. Ernest, Rebecca, and Ilse stayed in the kitchen while their home was being ransacked by the demons. The soldiers went to the backyard. Rebecca looked out the window to see if they were going near the woodpile. One went close enough to kick at the wood. Some of the wood fell. When the wood fell, a sharp piece fell on the top of Eva's head. She began to bleed. She never moved. She never made a sound. She knew if she did, they would kill her and Ilse's family for hiding her. She stayed frozen in place watching them through the tiny holes in between the stacked wood. Their pounding footsteps through the tiny backyard was petrifying to her heart. She thought she was going to explode with fear. She imagined they must have been the SS that killed Edgar. She began to cry. Her tears froze on her cheeks. She knew she needed to stop crying or they might hear her. Finally, she saw bits and pieces of their uniforms moving back into the back door that led to the kitchen.

Ernest stood up as they moved into the kitchen. "We will inform you if we see anyone out of the ordinary in this area," he stated in their native tongue.

"Heil Hitler," the soldier that was in charge said with a Nazi salute.

Ernest could not bring himself to respond back with a "Heil Hitler" response. He showed them to the front door and locked it as fast as he could. He watched them get into a huge black military car. They sped down the street. When they were out of sight, Ernest told Rebecca to get Eva and make she was warm. Rebecca ran to the back yard and pulled Eva out of the wood pile. She saw the blood on her head. Dirt and sawdust had fallen on her face. Tears had run down her cheeks and made frozen streaks through the dirt and sawdust.

"Oh, child, you've been through so much. What have they done to you?" Rebecca asked.

"A piece of wood fell on my head when they kicked the wood pile. It's all right. They didn't find me, and they didn't harm you. This will heal," Eva answered holding the knot on the top of her head with agony that she did not want to show. She did not want to scare Ilse any more than she was. She had been through enough. They all had.

"Ilse, can you get a hot bath started for Eva?" Rebecca asked, hoping Ilse was not too traumatized.

Ilse immediately ran upstairs to draw the bath.

"I will go to the bar and see if Jalvja is here yet. We need to get her out of here as soon as possible," Ernest said. "Plus, I could use a drink or ten."

"I understand, my love." Rebecca kissed him on his way out the front door.

"I'll be back soon," Ernest reassured her.

"We'll get her ready for the trip," Rebecca stated with confidence of what to do to keep everyone safe.

Four hours later Ernest came back home. Eva was packed and ready to go whenever this Jalvja person arrived.

Eva was dressed in the warmest clothes that they could provide. Teresa and Bruce loved cross country skiing. Rebecca and Ernest gave her some of Teresa's skiing clothes so she would stay warm while crossing over to Scotland. She was also given one of Teresa's dresses and a pair of practical shoes, so she could use it while looking for a job in NYC.

Chapter Twenty-One

Jalvja

Music: "Little Brown Jug" Glenn Miller
"Oh Johnny, Oh Johnny, Oh!" Orrin Tucker & his Orchestra
History: January 7, 1940 Rationing of basic food is established in the UK
Ernest came back from the bar with good news. Jalvja was in town. He had been in town for two days. His whiskey sales around town were almost done. His stops in the red-light district were completed. The Amsterdam liquor that he usually traded for was not as abundant because of the shortages of the political climate. He would have more room on his forty-foot fishing boat than usual. He was willing to take Eva on board, but they would have to sneak her on board at the very last minute, and it would have to be during the busiest time of day so that she would go unnoticed. She would have to dress like a man to get to the docks.

Eva understood what she had to do. She left the Dekkers' home. She had fallen in love with each of them. She would stay in touch with them for the rest of their lives. She promised to write as soon as she got to New York. They cried, hugged. She snuck out of the house the next day at three o'clock in the afternoon. She would blend in with the fishermen and dock workers. Ernest gave her the directions to Jalvja's slip. She had to follow them perfectly to get there as fast as possible. Jalvja would have the motor running. They would have to leave immediately. Jalvja knew both of their lives, and his two mates' lives would be in terrible danger if they were caught with a refugee from Germany on board. It's especially dangerous that she is a known traitor.

Eva was smart enough to not run through the streets to her rescuer. Ernest told her to go at a quick pace but do not run. Running would cause suspicion and draw attention.

The docks were near. Seagulls were flying above. Salty air was palatable. Eva could see the pier where Jalvja's boat was docked. She had to cross one more pedestrian bridge before she could board it. She was so close. She could see the stocky man with the beard on the deck of the fishing boat from Scotland. It was a bright yellow boat. It reminded her of Papa's delivery truck. She started to tear up because of that memory. She knew she had to control herself to get through this. There was no time for crying.

Jalvja's long red beard was blowing in the breeze. The smoke from his pipe was trailing off into the harbor. He was pacing as if he was ready to get his boat out to sea. She caught his eye. Jalvja was wise and perceptive. Although she was dressed like a man, he knew it was her by her body language.

Suddenly, she saw a troop of Nazi soldiers arrive on the pedestrian bridge that separated them. She froze in place. The soldiers were checking people as they went across the bridge. She ducked into an alley and hid behind trash bins. She was so afraid that she peed down her leg. The good thing about that was that it warmed her up. The bad thing about that was that it would eventually freeze her pants to her legs as she crouched behind the bins. She saw Jalvja come over the bridge towards her. She had no idea what was about to happen. She was afraid for him. She did not realize he was a force to be reckoned with. He had a plan to get her safely on his boat. He hoped she was bright enough to figure it out instantly and go along with it. Both of their lives depended on it. He started by yelling at her as if she were a disobedient scallywag deckhand that needed to get on the boat and stop slacking.

"Boy... get that bag and get on that boat before I beat you," Jalvja shouted at Eva.

Frightened enough to go along with the demands of this strange man, she picked up a bag that was laying in the alley and hoisted it and her measly bag of possessions over her shoulder. Both bags covered her face. She tried to walk like a man so as not to give herself away to the Nazi's.

Jalvja pretended to kick her in the pants and she played along with it. The Nazis had already checked him out. They knew he was the captain of his boat. He looked angry and unapproachable. They did not bother to ask for the vagrant's identification. They could see he belonged to the captain. The deckhand was receiving enough of a beating that they did not need to intervene. The situation was handling itself. Fortunately, Jalvja's risky plan was working.

Jalvja yelled violently at Eva all the way across the bridge so they would not be disturbed by the soldiers.

"You disobedient son of a bitch. I told you to be on time," Jalvja continued his rebuke of this insubordinate worker.

Eva cringed as he yelled at her. She was glad that he was able to get her past the Nazis. She was terrified that he might really be this mean. What did she get herself into?

With one last pretend kick in the arse, Eva bounced onto the deck. This was either the craziest thing she had ever done or the smartest. It was yet to be determined. Jalvja gave the signal to the first mate and they were off without anyone bothering to stop them.

Eva dropped all the things she was carrying onto the deck. She looked at the man that had just scared her to death and saved her life at the same time.

"I'm Eva." She stuck out her hand to shake Jalvja's hand, not knowing what his reaction might be. If he was still going to kick her in the arse, she figured she was still close enough to shore she could jump off the deck and swim to shore.

Jalvja told her to go below deck. He did not want to have anyone on shore seeing anything that might put them in danger.

Once below deck, Jalvja stuck out his hand too and gently shook hers. Then he took her hand and kissed it as if she was royalty. She was pleasantly pleased. She could not take another terrifying moment.

Joe and Jason were already leaving the dock. They knew it was of utmost urgency to leave as soon as possible.

"I'm Jalvja. The Dekkers told me all about you. I'm so very sorry for all you've been through. We will get you to Scotland safely. Then you can board a ship from Edinburgh to America. Do you have enough money to get passage to America? If not, we can help you with that too," Jalvja said.

"Yes, I think I have enough to get me through to New York. I have someone meeting me at a place called Ellis Island. Does that sound familiar to you?" Eva asked.

"Yes, that is the port that all immigrants go through. You will register there. Let's get you settled. There's a tiny bunk on the port side of the boat. It's not much, but it's clean. Can you cook?" Jalvja asked.

"A little," Eva answered.

"Good," Jalvja chuckled his deep comforting laugh, "We're tired of our cooking, aren't we, boys?" The two crewmates, Joe and Jason, laughed in agreement. "Get settled in and we'll introduce you to the galley. Sound all right?"

"Yes, sounds good. Glad to help in any way I can. I'm so grateful for your kindness," Eva answered.

Jalvja knew the best thing for her would be to keep busy. She had been through so much lately. She needed to feel useful and as normal as possible. She made a grand supper for the crew. Fresh fish, fried potatoes, vegetables that Jalvja had picked up while in Amsterdam. Then of course the crew cracked open the finest alcohol that they had purchased while in Amsterdam. After dinner they set the course for the boat to dock in Edinburgh. The crew of three drank, played cards, and told colorful stories and jokes that made Eva blush. They adopted her as their little sister immediately. She felt very cared for, and she cared for them. She tried their whiskey. She could only down one shot. She spewed most of it out and turned green. She was getting a bit seasick on the choppy waves. Her land legs had never experienced this kind of waviness before. She finished cleaning the galley and listening to their stories then headed to her tiny bunk. She grabbed a bucket to take with her. She felt like she would be throwing up a lot, and she did.

By morning, when the crew was coming into port at Edinburgh, Eva had vomited so much that Jalvja was overly concerned for her. She reassured him that she would be fine. It was just seasickness. She did not look well.

Jalvja had business in Edinburgh with many of the bars. Joe and Jason would go with him for deliveries and take in some card games and brothels around town. They would not be back until dark.

"Will you be all right, Lass? We've got business to attend to. Stay below deck. This is a rough area," Jalvja warned Eva.

"I'll be all right. I'm sure it was just seasickness. I'll have dinner on for you boys when you get back," Eva insisted.

Jalvja, Joe, and Jason unloaded the liquor onto the delivery truck they kept at port. Jalvja had a bad feeling about leaving Eva alone on the ship. If she stayed below deck, she would be fine.

"Lads, we need to get deliveries done quickly. I don't like the idea of the lass on the boat by herself," Jalvja insisted of his crew.

"Not a problem, sir," Jason answered, understanding his concern.

"Ya won't get to see Miss Kate tonight, Jason. She'll be disappointed missin' your wee willy," Joe said with a shot to the arm.

"She'll have ta wait for a few days. It'll make her want me more," Jason said jokingly.

"Aye, if'n it don't shrink up and fall off due to no one usin' it," Joe joked and threw a case at him to load onto the truck.

"Aye, then yours must've fallen off years ago," Jason said as he punched him back with a jousting verbal brotherly blow.

"All right, ya two," Jalvja said, laughing with them, "let's get on with it. I'm worried about our little lass. We've got to get her situated on a ship going to America.

As the mates went around the pubs, they asked about any ships that might be heading to America. One of the pubs had a commercial ship docked that would be leaving in two days to America. Jalvja would ask Eva if that would be an option for her. They might even pay her if she could work while on the ship. He did not want to send her on a ship that had a rough crew. He would check out the passenger ships in the area too.

It was almost dusk. The pubs were filling up with business and getting rowdy. Their deliveries were done. Back to their vessel and a home-cooked meal that Eva had promised. They parked the truck near the shipyard and began walking the few blocks to their slip. Suddenly, they heard screaming. They all took off running as fast as they could, hoping it was not Eva.

Eva had come up to the bow to get some fresh air. She had been below deck all day, just as Jalvja told her to. The rocking of the boat made her unnaturally nauseated. She was so seasick that she needed to come up for air. She could not prepare their meal. Weak as a kitten. Limp as a rag. She hung her head over the port side of the boat and vomited until there was nothing left to vomit.

Two Russian sailors from a nearby commercial ship had spotted her and came over to kidnap her onto their ship and rape her. She was being pulled down the pier by these oversized goons. All she could do was belt out a weak little scream. She was too weak to fight them off.

Jalvja, Joe, and Jason heard screaming. They realized it was Eva. They ran up the pier to save her. Jalvja was the first one to get to them. He punched the first one so hard that he fell off the pier and into the water. Joe and Jason punched the second one. They got him away from Eva while Jalvja picked her up in his arms and carried her quickly back to his vessel. She lay in his arms like a rag doll. There was barely any life left in her. Her long hair draped over his huge muscular right arm. Her limp body barely breathing.

The Russian that Joe and Jason were fighting had pulled a knife on them. Joe pulled a knife out and thrust it into his gut. The Russian fell off the pier toward the other kidnapper. Joe and Jason ran down the pier and to their boat. They started the engine and got out of port as fast as possible.

Jalvja carried Eva to her berth and put her down gently. Joe and Jason knew they needed to move quickly before the entire Russian crew came down on them. They had rushed to untie from the dock. As the boat moved away from its' moorings Jalvja pondered what to do with Eva. She could not travel to America in this bad of shape.

"North to Pittenweem, boys. I think we need to give this lass a few days' rest at home on solid ground. Head to my Mum's house. We'll have her look at her," Jalvja commanded his crew.

"Yes, sir," they answered.

Pittenweem, Scotland, was their next stop, a safe little fishing village on the Eastern coast. Jalvja lived next door to his mother and Father. Since losing his wife and son on a fishing trip in a bad storm, he has never remarried. His parents, siblings, and many nephews and nieces live in the small fishing village. His family has been there for generations. They all have something to do with the fishing industry. His fishing crew, Joe and Jason, are distant cousins. They have known Jalvja like an older brother all their lives. They have never seen him this worried since losing his wife and son.

Eva's little body and mind was about to collapse. Jalvja would lay on the floor next to her berth until they arrived and docked at his home port. Like a mother bear he watched to make sure she was still breathing. Her breaths were shallow. Her skin was pale. She had been roughed up by those Russian sailors. She might have internal injuries or broken bones. She would wake for moments at a time throughout the trip, only to dry heave in her unconscious state. Then go back to sleeping.

Chapter Twenty-Two

Pittenweem, Scotland

Music: "We're Going to Hang Out the Washing on the Siegfried Line" Jimmy Kennedy

"You're a Sweet Little Headache" Bing Crosby

History: January 21, 1940: U-boat sinks British destroyer *HMS Exmouth* and its crew of 135 are all lost.

They made good time. Joe and Jason could see the lighthouse and the shore lights of Pittenweem. They yelled down to Jalvja to let him know they would be docking soon. Once they docked, he wrapped Eva in some wool blankets and carried her off the ship and down the dock to his parent's home. It was late. They would be sleeping. He knew they would not care. As he carried her limp body to the front door he knocked and pushed the door open with his foot. He turned on the light of the kitchen and yelled upstairs for Mum and Dad.

"Mum, I need some help here," Jalvja yelled up the stairwell to their bedroom in their cottage.

"We're coming, boy, we're coming. What the bloody hell are ya doin' getting us up this late at night? What could be this important to disturb your old parents? We mighta been gettin' a wee bit of lovin' in, ya know?" Jalvja's father said with a laugh and an ornery grin as he came down the stairs in front of his mother, both in their pajamas and robes.

"Oh, Daddy, Jalvja doesn't want to hear that nonsense," Jalvja's mother said as she smacked Father on the arse.

Then both parents saw Jalvja had a person in his arms, a very ill person. They both gasped with surprise.

"For gawd's sakes, Jalvja, who is this?" Father asked.

"Put her over here on the sofa," Mother said as she tossed the pillows and a cat off the couch to fit this poor weak child on it.

"Her name is Eva. I picked her up from Amsterdam. One of my clients was helping her escape Europe," Jalvja answered as he lay her gently down and covered her with blankets. "Her husband was shot for being a deserter and traitor. My client's daughter and son-in-law were in the way and helping them hide. The Nazis shot them too."

"I can't imagine the distress she has been through," Mum said as she put a kettle on for tea.

"That's not all, Mum," Jalvja continued, "She got very seasick on our way over here. Then when we were docked in Edinburgh and we were doing deliveries, some Russian sailors had drug her off the boat and were kidnapping her. I'm not sure if she might've been raped!"

"We need to get her to the doctor first thing in the morning," Father said.

"Meanwhile, I'll drop some fluids into her until morning with a sponge. We've got to keep her hydrated," Mum insisted. "You get some rest. I'll take care of her."

"I'm not going anywhere. The boys are taking care of the rest of my deliveries and business. I'll stay with her too. I'll sleep right here on the floor," Jalvja insisted.

"That will work," Father said, seeing the grave concern on Jalvja's face. "I'll go back to bed. Call me if you need anything. We'll drive her to the doctor first thing in the morning."

"Yes. We'll get you up in a few hours, sweetheart," Mother answered.

Mum and Jalvja took turns throughout the night dripping water into Eva's mouth. She could only take a few drops at a time.

When the sun was rising over the little fishing village, Father went to get the truck ready for transporting Eva to their doctor. Mum stayed home and got some rest. Jalvja sat on the passenger side while Father drove. Eva was wrapped in wool blankets, her head on Jalvja's lap. They were at the doctor's office for a few hours. An IV was started. It perked Eva up to the point of waking up and talking a little, still groggy.

"Where am I?" Eva woke and asked of Jalvja.

He had fallen asleep waiting for her to wake.

"Eva! So glad you're awake. We've been so worried about you," Jalvja said. "You're in Pittenweem, Scotland."

Eva laughed, "That's a funny name. You're making that up, aren't you?"

Jalvja laughed. It was so good to hear her laugh. So good to hear her at all.

"It is a funny name. It's a beautiful name to me," Jalvja said, "It's my hometown. I've brought you here because you have been gravely sick."

"I told you it was just seasickness," Eva said, wondering why he was so worried.

The doctor entered the room.

"Right. Well, it was more than that," the Doctor began to explain. "The lump on your head from the Nazis, I think that gave you a bit of a concussion. Your skin is open to infection because of the dragging marks on your back and legs from the Russian pirates. You'll have to keep those areas very clean. I don't know what they dragged you through. As far as I can tell, you did not get raped. You got lucky. The distress that you have been facing these past weeks over your husband's death, being on the run, and seasickness, all of this has added up to a lot of stress on your body. I imagine you haven't been eating too well?"

"Right, it's been hard too after Edgar's death. And before that it was hard when we were in hiding," Eva said. "I still don't have an appetite."

"Well, that makes sense. There's one more thing that you need to know. Another thing that has added to the stress on your body." The doctor slowly approached. "You are pregnant."

Eva was sitting on the examination table. She doubled over with excitement and trepidation. Tears immediately welled up in her eyes. Tears of happiness and then tears of fear.

Jalvja teared up too. How happy this news must be for her. She will still have a part of her husband with her. She must get healthy so she can carry this baby. His family could help her through this, if she wanted their help.

"I can't believe it. I'm pregnant?" Eva cried, putting her face in her hands and then in her lap. So many feelings were pouring out of her. She could not be happier. She could not be more afraid.

Jalvja and the doctor let her cry it out. The doctor handed her a box of tissues to wipe her tears away. He and Jalvja were wiping their own tears away. It was the happiest Eva had been since her wedding day. She wanted to call home and tell everyone. The doctor had a phone. She tried to call Edgar's parents. No answer. There was no answer at the butcher shop or the Schwartzes either.

"I'll write them. They will all be so happy," Eva exclaimed, "I can't believe this. I have a little piece of Edgar to keep with me. He would be so happy."

The Doctor warned her, "You need to take better care of yourself to get this baby to full term. You are underweight and not very strong right now. You need to think about your next steps and what you will do."

"You can stay with me and my family until you decide to go to America or Hungary," Jalvja offered.

Eva stuttered in disbelief and joy, "That is such a generous offer. I… I don't know what to say. I must make decisions for the two of us now. Let me think about it. Doctor, how far along am I?"

"Not too far along. Maybe six to eight weeks."

"Let's go back to my parents' home. We'll talk about things there. We can get you a nice hot meal and figure things out," Jalvja encouraged.

Eva hugged the doctor for taking such good care of her. He reciprocated with a smile and a big hug back.

"I can't pay you anything right now. I will remember your kindness always. Thank you so much for such wonderful news," Eva said with deep appreciation.

"No need for payment, Lass. You are most welcome. I'm glad to give you some good news. You deserve some good news," Doctor McLaughlin answered.

Jalvja assisted her out to the truck where his father was waiting. They drove back to his parents' home. The whole family was there: sisters, brothers, cousins, aunts and uncles, nieces, and nephews. Jalvja was not expecting the entire community to be there. He assisted Eva out of the truck. They walked up to the house and walked into a large gathering. It was like one of their Christmas gatherings. Lots of chattering and laughing going on.

"Whoa, what the hell are all of you doing here?" Jalvja said with a mighty roar and a laugh. It was so good to see everyone, "Is it Christmas?"

Jalvja threw his arm around the nearest nephew and rubbed his head with his knuckles until he screamed, "UNCLE!"

All the nieces ran up to him wanting their turn from him to throw them up in the air and catch them.

His three sisters got in line to get their favorite oldest brother's hugs and a twirl. His four younger brothers queued up to see who had the strongest handshake. Jalvja still had it.

Everyone had brought food as if it were a holiday. Mother and Father had told them about Eva. They wanted to meet her and help her in any way they could.

"I suppose ya want to meet Miss Eva?" Jalvja shouted over the friendly mob in the living room, "This is Mrs. Eva Holthaus."

Everyone cheered and said their hellos collectively. She felt like she was back at the mansion with Edgar's big loving family.

"Thank you, thank you," Eva said as the crowd quieted down.

Jalvja nodded to Eva and asked her permission to tell her news.

She nodded back with a resounding yes.

"We've got some news to tell ya," Jalvja began.

"What is it, ya big bag of wind?" Father quipped. Everyone laughed. They knew Jalvja was one to talk on and on for hours.

"We just came back from the doctors. It wasn't just seasickness the lass had," Jalvja began.

"It was probably the rotten food ya carry on that tortured old boat of yours," one of Jalvja's brothers, Ronnie, yelled out from the back of the room. "I've been sick many times on his boat, Eva. We understand."

Everyone roared with laughter.

"See if I ever bring you back any Amsterdam liquor, Ronnie," Jalvja poked back and laughed with the rest of them, knowing it was partially true about the bad food.

"Shush your mouths for a second. We've got some great news for ya. Eva is carrying a child from her late husband Edgar," Jalvja announced.

The cheering and screaming and congratulations went on for a long time. Everyone was overwhelmed with excitement for Eva. Everyone offered her help with whatever she needed. She could not have felt more love if she had been back home in Tokaj. The entire clan seemed to usher her over to the sofa where she could rest and be comfortable. It felt like she was floating on a cloud with all of the helping hands guiding her.

The family calmed down after a while and dug into a nice hearty meal together. Afterwards the clanging of dishes being washed by the women filled the home with sounds of normal. Eva was thankful for these sounds.

The men went outside to smoke. They were talking of all they could do for Eva. They were willing to do whatever she needed. Conversations turned to all the work they needed to do on their boats. There was always work to be done on the boats.

The ladies had Eva sit in the living room and rest. She felt like a queen. They were an astonishing family. She could see herself staying in Pittenweem and raising her child here. It was such a loving cozy atmosphere. She was not sure if she should go on to New York or not. She did know that she could not go back to Hungary until the war was over. Even then, what would she find?

"We will put you up in a bedroom upstairs, Eva. Would that be all right?" Mother asked.

"That is more than all right, Mrs. McMilam. I will help around the house to pay my way. Please tell me what I can do," Eva answered.

"Jeanette, my dear, just call me Jeanette. My husband's name is Tim. You can rest for right now. You need to get stronger. There will be plenty of work to do as soon as you're strong enough," Jeanette answered.

Weeks passed. Eva felt right at home with the McMilam family. If she could contribute her fair share of work, she thought she could continue here for the duration of the war, then go back home. She felt she would have two homes. Her English was getting better. She had to listen earnestly because of their thick Scottish brogue. She would catch on. They were doing their best to learn some Hungarian too.

When Jalvja was away on his import and export trips to Europe she stayed in his home. The entire family lived within a ten-mile radius of one another. Eva loved how close they were.

Two months passed and Eva was over her morning sickness. Her daily routine was to clean Jalvja's home and help Jeanette cook. She wrote letters to Ilse and her family in Germany and Hungary. Jalvja was able to deliver the letters to Ilse's family. They were overjoyed that Eva was pregnant. They sent Edgar's viola and cremated remains back with Jalvja the next time he delivered. Her Hungarian family may not have been getting her letters. They were not answering her phone calls either. She was very worried about what was happening there. The McMilams and she would listen to the radio for updates about the war. There were no updates about Tokaj. They were just general updates about the war.

Jalvja gave Eva the large bedroom in his cottage. It was upstairs and overlooked the bay. He knew she loved to paint. As she looked out the bay window under the thatched roof onto the endless ocean, she was able to paint some incredible paintings. She gave Dr. McLaughlin one of her paintings to repay him. She gave each of Jalvja's siblings a painting. She also sent some paintings back with Jalvja to Amsterdam to see if she could sell them in some of the shops. She signed them in an alias, J.J. Lena, so she would not be traced by the Nazis. She was becoming well-known as a great artist in Pittenweem and in Amsterdam. She wondered if she could sell her paintings and make a living doing it.

Eva felt safe. She thought she would stay in Scotland and maybe, when the war was over, move her grandparents here where they could be safe too.

Then, for some unknown reason she looked at Edgar's viola sitting there quietly across the room where she had been painting. She missed him so very very much. She wanted to feel close to him again. The box of his ashes was sitting next to the viola.

"Oh," she said with anger and tears, "why can't you magically appear and play your viola for me? Why did you have to go?" She paused, walked over and dropped to the floor next to the instrument. She grabbed the ashes into her chest and hugged them. "I miss you. I miss you so much." She sobbed uncontrollably until she was exhausted. She lay down on the floor, still hugging the box of ashes and cried for him. "Edgar… Edgar… we're going to have a baby. I'll name him after you if it's a boy. Be with me through this. Please be with me."

Her tortured heart was lost. She was happy here in Scotland. But she missed Edgar so deeply. She missed her family. She missed their dreams. After a while, she sat up. She opened his viola case. It lay there looking beautiful but as dead as Edgar was. Only he could play this instrument as eloquently as it deserved. There would never be another prodigy like him. They killed him, and for what? He was no traitor. He was just trying to keep himself and me safe. She took the viola and the bow out of the case. She put it to her shoulder, just like he would have done. She stroked the bow over the strings. It sounded horrible. She had no talent. But it was as close to hearing his voice as she could get. She played it for a while until she got tired of hearing her awful playing.

"You, poor viola, you've never sounded so bad. I apologize to you. You miss him too, don't you?" Eva laughed at herself for striking up a conversation with Edgar's viola.

She had never looked in the little compartment where he kept the extra strings. She turned the little clasp that was holding the velvet-covered door down and saw something that was unexpected. It was not extra strings. It was an envelope. She opened it. There was a folded piece of paper inside it. She unfolded it. It was two pieces of paper. There was a short note written on it. When she unfolded it completely, there were several dried rosebuds.

The note said, "For our one-year anniversary, I collected these rosebuds from the night of our honeymoon. They are to remind you of my love for you that will last forever. Our dreams have come true. We are together. Let us go wherever our dreams lead us and always be on our honeymoon. I love you truly, my rosebud," signed "Edgar."

Eva fell backwards into the pillows on the floor. She cried uncontrollably and thought to herself, "I miss you so much my love. You're telling me to fulfill our dreams. What does that mean at this point in our lives?"

She needed time to think of what he really wanted for her and now for their little one. What is the best direction for her to go?

She decided to paint. It was the only thing that really cleared her mind. She sat for hours looking out the bay window onto the rough winter Scottish sea that was battering the beautiful docks and stone sea walls of Pittenweem.

As she sat and painted the darting seagulls, massive stone harbor, colorful fishing boats, crashing winter waves, she also noticed an old spider's web dangling from the overhanging red tile roof onto her outside windowsill. She stopped looking at scenery far away and began to look at the scenery that was close at hand. The old, tattered spider's web was beautiful even in its diminished state. It had been there a while. It was torn, dusty, barely hanging on to the roof's red tiles and the shallow windowsill. But… it was still hanging on. Even in the cold, windy, winter weather it was strong enough to hang on. How could it be so strong to hang on through the harsh weather, wind, rain, and snow that it had faced since being woven there by some talented, dedicated spider? It brought back memories of the spider web that Edgar fell on when they first met. Eva laughed thinking about that day. She still hated spiders, yet she could not help but be amazed at the beauty that they create with their webs. Then out of nowhere a tiny snowflake landed on the sooty, dangling web. The intricacy and beauty of just one fragile snowflake was magical. Every snowflake is unique. Every life is unique. The combination of the snowflake on the spider's web gave Eva her answer.

Life is fragile, fleeting, complicated, dangerous, full of beauty and intricate details, delicately intertwined, like a snowflake on a spider's web.

I must be strong, brave, careful and powerful to survive this life. It is up to me to do this for us. She held her tummy to let their baby know what she now understands. She looked at Edgar's viola to let him know that she would not let him down. Especially now that she is carrying their baby. She would do her best to make the right decisions for all of them.

She would move on to fulfill her and Edgar's dreams. She knew she had to. It was their hope, to be safe and live free.

That night at dinner with Jeanette and Tim, Eva brought up the subject, "What do you think of me going to New York?"

The couple looked at each other and thought a few minutes.

"If you want to go, you, of course, have our blessing," Tim said.

"You have our blessing in whatever you do, my dear. You've become family, like a daughter to us, now. Tell us what your plans are, and we will help you do whatever you want to do," Jeanette said with a heavy heart. She and Tim gave each other that look that any parent would give a child if they were taking on more than they could handle.

"It was Edgar's wish to go to America and be safe from the war, to start a new life there away from hatred and prejudice. I think the symphony would help me at least get established. I have our savings with me. I can work and sell my paintings," Eva said.

"You are a hard worker, but who would help you with this child?" Jeanette asked, patting her now growing tummy.

"True, good question. I would have to find friends that could help me with that. The Jewish community would be a safe place for me and the baby. It will be easier for me to travel and get set up before I have the baby," Eva said, still seeking the right direction for her and the baby.

"Whichever way you go, we will help you," Tim said, with Jeanette shaking her head in agreement. "You will always be welcome here if it does not work out there."

"Oh, thank you so very much. You are family to me now too. I will start packing my bags tonight. I won't leave until Jalvja gets back. I will want to tell him face-to-face before I go," Eva said with relief.

Chapter Twenty-Three

Onward

Music: "God Bless America" Irving Berlin / Kate Smith
"Sunrise Serenade" Glenn Miller

History: January 24, 1940: Reinhard Heydrich is appointed by German General Göring for the solution to the "Jewish Question."

February 15, 1940 Hitler orders unrestricted submarine warfare.

During World War II the United States began making changes to its policy of immigration quotas, generally on a case-by-case basis. In 1939 a well-publicized plight of Jewish refugees from Europe aboard the *SS St. Louis* first were refused permission to disembark in Cuba, then denied permission to emigrate to the United States. Because of strict immigration quotas in force at the time, Roosevelt had no choice but to refuse to accept these refugees and the ship was turned back to Europe. In 1944 President Franklin Roosevelt, under pressure from Congress and Jewish Americans, relaxed the quotas on Eastern European immigration to allow more Jews to immigrate and escape Nazi persecution. He also created a War Refugee Board to allow more refugees entry into the United States. Jewish immigrants after 1944 settled largely in cities.

Jalvja, Joe, and Jason came back from Amsterdam a few days later. He had sold two of Eva's paintings to some wealthy collectors. He was excited to give her the money. He had also been thinking of Eva and the baby. He could give them security and a permanent home. He could love her and the baby. She was ten years younger than he was. He did not know how she would feel about marrying an old sailor. He thought about approaching the matter when he got back in port.

The Sunrise, Jalvja's boat, docked in Pittenweem. It was painted yellow because Abigail, his deceased wife, loved sunrises and the color yellow.

The crew could not be happier to be home. It had been a taxing trip. The weather had made the seas choppier than they had ever seen. The increased war action had made the maneuvering at their normal destinations complicated to navigate. Large battleships from allied forces were exhausting to navigate around. Increased Nazi presence in Amsterdam made it almost impossible to do business. He thought it would be best to wait until safer traveling times before he did anymore whiskey trade. He would stay close to home and fish for a while. Sell locally and in the Highlands. This would also give him a chance to know Eva better.

He opened the door to his parents' house and walked in, as was his nature. Eva and Jeanette were cooking supper in the kitchen. Her little belly had popped out even more than when he had last seen her. She was adorable. His father was putting more wood in the wood stove. It smelled so good. It smelled like home.

"Jalvja!" Mother said with a cheerful voice. "You're home safe again."

"Yes, Mother, so good to see you." Jalvja picked her up by the waist, gave her a big hug, and twirled her around the kitchen. "I'll be staying in port for a while. It's getting rough out there."

"How so, boy?" Father said, as he shook his hand and gave him a hearty hug.

"Seas are rough. Increased military on the waters. Increased Nazis in Amsterdam," Jalvja answered, "I'll stay here and do some fishing. Trade locally. The Dekkers are doing well. They send all their love to you, Eva. I'm glad we got you out when we did. I don't think it could've been possible now."

Jalvja took a good look at Eva. She was looking so much healthier. There was a glow to her pretty face. Her beautiful long glistening black hair was tied back with a cotton scarf. She was wearing one of Jeanette's aprons. Her smile brightened up the whole kitchen. She was perfect.

"How are you, young lady?" He gave her a huge hug and a twirl, just as if she were one of the girls in his family. "I'd better set you down gently," he said looking at her tummy. "How's the baby?"

She giggled as he set her down gently.

"I'm doing great. The baby's not making me throw up anymore. We're both doing very well. Thanks to you and your lovely family," she answered with a bright loving smile. "I do have something I want to tell you."

"And what's that?" Jalvja asked, not knowing it was going to be a severe bombshell.

"I've decided to continue on to New York," Eva stated with enthusiasm, not knowing she just pierced his heart.

Jalvja's heart sunk. He tried not to show it. His parents knew it was going to hurt him. They had secretly talked about how nice it would be if Jalvja and Eva would get together. It would fill an empty void in both of their hearts.

"You are?" Jalvja asked, squelching his disappointment. He did not know what to say. He had a speech planned for her, in private, to see what she thought about staying and getting to know each other better.

"Yes, I feel better now. I was looking through some of Edgar's things, and I found a note that he meant to give to me for our first anniversary. It is clear what I need to do after considering the plans that we had both made," Eva explained.

"Well, we will help you do whatever you need to do," Jalvja sighed and nodded his head to agree with whatever she needed.

"That's what we told her too, son," Tim added. "She is always welcome to come back here. She is family now."

"Of course, she is," Jeanette added. "We will miss you terribly. You will always have a home here."

"I'm already packed. Where should I leave from? What would be the safest route?" Eva asked Jalvja.

"I would go via train to Edinburgh. Catch a passenger ship there to America. The waters are choppy. You sure you're over being sick?" Jalvja said, with deep concern for this risky decision.

"I'll be all right. If I leave soon, I will keep your family from getting in harm's way. I will write. I will keep you informed of all that I'm doing. I'll be fine," Eva said. She looked straight into Jalvja's eyes. She had a feeling of what he was thinking by the way he was looking at her. It only firmed up her resolve to go to America even more. She could not let him fall in love with her. That was not in her plans. He was an incredible man. He would take care of her and the baby, but he was not her destiny.

"When will you leave?" Jalvja asked.

"I'll give it two days. I'll need to say goodbye to everyone. I'll try to call my family in Düsseldorf and Hungary once more before I leave. I will try to call the New York City Symphony's number again too," Eva answered.

"I'll take you to the train station," Jalvja offered.

"Thank you very much. I appreciate all you have done for me and the baby. I love you, your family, and Pittenweem," Eva said as she hugged him tightly.

She wanted him to know that she loved him and appreciated everything that he and his family had done. He knew. He felt it in her hug.

Two days later Eva was at the closest phone for the village, the post office. She still could not get through to Düsseldorf or Hungary. She did get through to a manager at the New York City Symphony. It was a short call, lots of static on the line. She could barely hear. She told the manager the whole situation. They were overwhelmingly interested in assisting her and the baby get settled in New York. There would be someone meeting her at Ellis Island when she arrived.

Jalvja's entire family came to Jeanette and Tim's home to say goodbye to Eva as she headed to the train station. Jalvja drove, in his old delivery truck, to the closest depot. They had a profoundly serious talk on the way there. He told her how he felt. She appreciated it with her whole heart.

"If by chance, things do not work out for me in America, we"—Eva pointed to her baby bump—"we will be back."

"I love you, Eva. You've stolen my heart. I will be here for whatever you need. Just say the word. When you get to Edinburgh, go see Charles and Jane at the Jolly Judge Pub. They will help you with everything. Tell them I sent you," Jalvja said with tears welling up in his eyes.

Eva started to cry too.

They hugged until the last train whistle blew. Jalvja kissed her on her precious cheek. It was all he could do. He wanted her and the baby to stay and be well taken care of by him and his family. He wanted to give her a long lingering kiss. It was not the right moment for that.

He helped her get the bags onto the train. He stood like a soldier, solid, protective of her, like a rock. Yet, a tear was falling and rolled down his cheek as the train began to move. She waved. Tears falling from her eyes too.

The train took her to Edinburgh. This train ride was different. This train ride was scary and lonely. At least there were no Nazi soldiers to worry about on this train ride. The only thing she had to hold onto was the promise of a free, but unknown, world ahead of her. It would be a world where she would raise their baby like Edgar would have wanted. The land of the free, the home of the brave awaited her arrival. Her courage barely outweighing her fear, she moved ahead, one step at a time.

Charles and Jane at the Jolly Judge Pub made Eva wonderfully comfortable at their home until she could catch the ship. She stayed with them for two days and enjoyed every minute of their Scottish hospitality.

The old, overcrowded passenger ship, that she bought tickets for, would take nearly two weeks to reach New York City. While on board Eva stayed to herself as much as possible. She feared there may be Nazi alliances lurking. She did not want to be caught unaware in case there were enemies aboard. She did not know who to trust.

The ship was packed with other refugees. Eva had a cheap bunk in the lowest level of the ship that she shared with three other young ladies and a baby boy. They were some of the lucky ones. Some people had to share their tiny bunks because of the overcrowding. She did not go too far from her bunk. What little she had, she did not want stolen, destroyed or eaten by the many rats. Her bunkmates seemed nice yet also fearful. They were all about the same age. Zdenka was from Croatia. Isabella was from Poland. They looked like they may have been through some of the war. Their eyes were full of fear and they were thin. As far as Eva could surmise, they seemed to be sisters or cousins. They did not speak Hungarian. Eva was friendly with them. They traded paper from their stationary for some food she shared with them. She did not need the stationary. However, she did not want to seem impolite. She had plenty of food packed for her by the McMilams, Charles and Jane. Eva hoped the best for them. That was all she felt safe to do. They were afraid and stand offish too.

The other young lady was from Germany. Eva could speak with her a little bit. She was Jewish. She had lost all her family in a violent attack from the SS. Her name was Alexa. Her two-year-old baby boy was the cutest baby Eva had ever seen. His name was Daxton. They had nothing to share or trade for food. They were the only survivors of their family. She had to be so strong to have gone through all she went through. They barely escaped with the clothes on their backs. Alexa scarcely had enough money for the passage for this ship. Some nuns came to her and Daxton's rescue with clothes and a little bit of money. Eva did not need to trade or accept anything from them. Charles and Jane's fresh baked bread and McMilam's dried cod helped sustain Alexa and Daxton until they reached the New York City harbor. Once they arrived at Ellis Island Alexa and Daxton would be picked up by their family from Ohio. Their lives would begin again. They would find peace in a safe place. Eva was hoping that for herself and all the terrified immigrants on the ship.

Thirteen days into the voyage, and the lights of the New York harbor were in sight. They were shining straight ahead of them, like multiple twinkling lighthouses. It was early morning. The sun was rising from the stern of the ship. Eva had gathered all her belongings and went to the bow. She found a quiet place to sit and hide on the deck. Her body was still in shadow as the sun rose from the east. The rising sun's rays were sparkling off the fathomless number of buildings that were ahead of them.

Then she saw her. Glistening like an angel in the harbor. Torch raised high. Welcoming the weary and heavy laden with an open heart. The Lady every immigrant thirsted to see, Lady Liberty. Like a lifeline, beckoning the tired and poor of the world into her safe harbor. Eva sat on the deck and wept uncontrollably.

She placed her hand on her tummy and spoke calming words to her unborn child, "This is it. This is our safe new home."

The ship came closer and closer to the beautiful statue. Eva stood, out of respect, to watch as the ship sailed right by this magnificent sign of safe haven. Eva could not take her eyes off her until they docked at Ellis Island.

Eva was met by several members of the string section of the New York City Symphony after she registered at Ellis Island. It took hours to get through the masses of people swarmed into the overwhelmed island. The artists waited patiently for her to arrive. The musicians, and now friends, took Eva to a safe home in the Bronx.

This began her new extraordinary life. She was home. She and her baby would be safe. Edgar would always be with them. He would have been so proud to have made it all the way to America. The wolf spider had devoured his innocent life. Eva had been set free.

WWII began September 1939. It ended September 1945.

Epilogue

Letters that were mailed but never received:
From Helena to Eva:

Dear Eva,

We hope you get this letter. We have not heard a word from you and Edgar since you left.

I married Samuel. We have had a baby boy. We named him Elijah. Emily married Daniel. They do not have any children.

The Nazis came after all the Jewish people in our area. Emily and I were hiding in our wine cellar when they came through. All of Edgar's cousins, except for Akos—he was too young—had already been sent to the front, and we heard they were killed. Since we are not Jewish by birth, we have been able to be spared. We tried to hide your family. The Nazis found them.

I am so sorry to tell you that the Nazis came through and took over the Schwartzes' winery. They used it as a base for a while. Your grandparents, the Schwartzes, Sandor and Rita and Akos were forced to kill all the livestock, including Lucy and Rocky. They had to butcher the livestock and cook for the Nazi soldiers.

*After the Nazis raided all the Jewish homes and stole all of
their art, jewelry, valuables, they lined up your
grandparents, the Schwartzes, and the winery staff and shot
them down on the vineyard's dock. They pushed them all
into the river after that. I am so sorry to have to write this
to you. I know you would want to know it from a friend
that you trust.*

*There are rumors around town about where the stolen art,
jewelry, and valuables have been taken to. It is in some
kind of "Gold Train." People are suspecting the Nazis
have hidden all of it in the mountains, possibly in Poland.*

I hope you and Edgar are safe.

*Please write when you can. This war has devastated all of
us. We hope it ends soon. We cannot take any more.*

*My family is well at this time. We are living off scarce
rations. We fear the future.*

*If America is safe and you think we should try to come
there, let us know.*

*All of my love,
Helena*

**One of the letters that Eva wrote to her and Edgar's family. It never
made it to them. None of her letters made it to them during the war.
She continued to write them and send them hoping they would somehow
get through.**

Dear Family,

*I am writing this same letter to each of you. All of you
need to know what has transpired. I have tried to call.
My calls have not been able to get through. I hope you
get this letter.*

Holocaust Memorial Museum (ushmm.org)

Spider's Web – Patti Laughlin Fogt

k): 978-1-6376-4333-4

© Patti Laughlin Fogt 2021

dersweb@gmail.com

rved No part of this publication may be reproduced
ny form or by any means, electronic or mechanical,
y, recording of any other information storage and
ithout prior written permission from the publisher.

Edgar and I left Düsseldorf by train for the Christmas Concert that the symphony was scheduled to play in Amsterdam. After the last concert, we escaped to a hiding place and waited for our ship to America to come in.

A week passed and the SS caught up with us. Edgar was so brave. He hid me in a hiding place that he made under the floorboards of our one-room, secret attic apartment. There was room enough for both of us. But he only had time to hide me. I am writing this with my heart broken to a thousand pieces and my life being now totally empty of my true love. The SS shot him for being a traitor and deserter.

I was helped by some local people to get through this. I had him cremated. He is with me now. The local people that helped me lost their daughter and son-in-law to the SS. Their granddaughter, Ilse, was hiding during the attack. She and I were the only survivors. We went to her grandparents' home. They helped me find a way to leave Amsterdam. They knew a man from Scotland, Jalvja. He brought me to Scotland, his hometown of Pittenweem.

I got very sick on the way over. I thought it was seasickness. Jalvja took me to the doctor in Pittenweem. I was seasick, but I am also pregnant. If it is a boy, I will name him Edgar, Jr. Jalvja and his family helped me get better.

I am sailing for America in a couple of days on a passenger ship from Edinburgh. The New York City Symphony has said they would help me get established, even though Edgar will not be with me.

This is the best route I think I should take at this time. I do hope you get this letter. If you do, please answer and mail it to the NYC Symphony address that I gave you.

All my love,
Eva

Life is fragile, complicated, dangerous, full of beauty and intricate details, delicately intertwined, like a snowflake on a spider's web. You must be strong, brave, careful, and powerful to survive this life. It is up to you.

Eva Holthaus – Holocaust Survivor
Tokaj, Hungary

United States F
Snowflake on a S
ISBN (paperba
Copyright text
snowflakeonaspi

All Rights Rese
or transmitted in a
including photocop
retrieval systems, w

To my entire family,
Corrie Leanne Fogt
incredible ladies. Th
are my sunshine and
From Ariel Ale
Alexa was beautiful
smile that could li
million mama bear
and always happy.
Daxton never
his face, and he w
To our Lou, twen
we had with you
missed the oppo
with all of your
Thanks to
from the Tokaj,
her video/ oral
you for sharin
survivor and t
search the Ur
Oral his
States Holo
go to: Unite